T G Trouper lives with his wife in Essex, England. He has one son that lives and works in America. He took up writing while still working in the live music industry, a job that he loved but had to leave to look after ailing parents. He still works part time in the industry, still building and preparing equipment for top musical artists. He is also a singer and guitarist in a couple of local bands.

This title, *The Twinmere Beast,* is his sixth release and the third in a series of horror-inspired stories.

Also by T G Trouper:

The Astrid series, female-led action thrillers:
Astrid book 1: War Changes People
Astrid book 2: Good People Do Bad Things
Astrid book 3: The Early Missions

The horror series:
Perfect Strangers
The Story, Be Careful What You Read

This work is dedicated to all those authors who are struggling to get their voices heard against the relentless tide of 'celebrity' publications. It is also dedicated to all those authors, who like me, use their own imagination, and refuse to have even one sentence of their work written for them by generative artificial intelligence.

T G Trouper

THE TWINMERE BEAST

AUSTIN MACAULEY PUBLISHERS
LONDON • CAMBRIDGE • NEW YORK • SHARJAH

Copyright © T G Trouper 2024

The right of T G Trouper to be identified as author of this work has been asserted by the author in accordance with sections 77 and 78 of the Copyright, Designs and Patents Act 1988.

All rights reserved. No part of this publication may be reproduced, stored in a retrieval system, or transmitted in any form or by any means, electronic, mechanical, photocopying, recording, or otherwise, without the prior permission of the publishers.

Any person who commits any unauthorised act in relation to this publication may be liable to criminal prosecution and civil claims for damages.

This is a work of fiction. Names, characters, businesses, places, events, locales, and incidents are either the products of the author's imagination or used in a fictitious manner. Any resemblance to actual persons, living or dead, or actual events is purely coincidental.

A CIP catalogue record for this title is available from the British Library.

ISBN 9781035865437 (Paperback)
ISBN 9781035865444 (ePub e-book)

www.austinmacauley.com

First Published 2024
Austin Macauley Publishers Ltd®
1 Canada Square
Canary Wharf
London
E14 5AA

Once again, I want to thank my wife, my sister, my good friends Sally, Julia, David, and fellow AM author Carley-Ann Osborn for their continued encouragement. I thank everyone else that appreciates my work, too many names to list here but you know who you are. I further thank Austin Macauley Publishers for their continued faith in my work.

Table of Contents

Chapter 1: The Storm	11
Chapter 2: The News	18
Chapter 3: The Lodge at Southmere	22
Chapter 4: Storytime	33
Chapter 5: The Search	45
Chapter 6: The Scale	47
Chapter 7: Father O'Sullivan	49
Chapter 8: The Beating	59
Chapter 9: Remains	66
Chapter 10: The Campaign	69
Chapter 11: The MP	80
Chapter 12: The Crossword	83
Chapter 13: Skeleton	101
Chapter 14: Similarities	108

Chapter 15: An Uncomfortable Thought   114

Chapter 16: The Letter   118

Chapter 17: A Trip to the Beach   128

Chapter 18: Christina   132

Chapter 1
The Storm

British Coastal Research vessel, the RV Neptune, sat stationary in the water two miles off the Suffolk coast and level with the abandoned village of Wychborough. Over the past ten years, relentless coastal erosion had eaten the cliffs away, undermining homes and destroying them. One hundred years ago, the village was a mile inland, but not anymore. No property was safe, and the last inhabitants had moved out of the village the previous year, never to return.

A severe storm the week before, coupled with the March high tide, had further eroded the sandy cliffs and a new set of empty houses teetered on the edge, waiting their turn to crash down the one hundred feet to join the homes, sheds, garages and greenhouses all shattered on the beach below. This was by far the greatest damage in living memory, and it had coincided with an international conference on sea defences, and as such, it had stayed in the news cycle for much longer than it otherwise would have done.

News crews, including international organisations from as far away as America and Australia, were getting as close as they could to the roped off areas on the beach, with the police constantly having to push them back. Other news crews were in what was left of Wychborough, interviewing various former residents, some distraught, some resigned to it and others angry. Local and national government figures were there making bland statements, skilfully crafting their meaningless comments to sound sympathetic but to also avoid saying anything that would leave them open to criticism or more importantly from their point of view, liability.

Some past occupants of the village were complaining about the local print media, berating the journalists for only paying attention now because there was international coverage. The gradual destruction had been going on for so long that up to this recent calamity, incidents often didn't even get reported. Those that did had at best two paragraphs sandwiched between the actions of vandals and the successes or failures of the local football team—that frequently took up four pages. A reporter from the local radio station skulked away from a now homeless resident, embarrassed when they had listed the amount of times they had sent emails to the station, only to not even receive an acknowledgement of receipt, let alone a reply.

Environmental protest groups had also arrived. These groups were keen to point out to anyone that would listen that the severity of the weather and the unusually high storm surge was the product of the global warming that they had been predicting for years. All of the groups, from the long standing and respected organisations, through to the newer fringe 'direct action' groups were present. And even though their methods were vastly different, one message was consistent across all of them: the threat from global warming that was causing the extreme weather events was real and no longer an issue that was out of sight and out of mind and happening to some country far away; it was directly affecting people in Britain and would only get worse. But their solutions to the problem were vastly different, ranging from a negotiated gradual reduction of fossil fuels while reliable alternatives were sought, through to demands to immediately cease all use of all fossil fuels everywhere in the world.

The most pressing issue, that of the coastal erosion problem, also caused divisions. Some argued that no matter what the underlying cause, it was a natural event so nothing should be done to protect the cliffs. Others had argued for defence, producing maps that showed the predicted attrition over the next one hundred years and the damage to critical infrastructure that it would cause. A couple of banner waving hyper-religious women claimed that it was God's work, and that man had no right to intervene. Others opposed the protection on financial grounds, claiming that the predictions were vastly exaggerated, while citing the enormous cost and potential futility of any such action. They argued that current proposed defensive methods would be wholly inadequate anyway, and their arguments were well thought out and convincing.

A small but very vocal group of climate change deniers had also taken up residence, and even they were divided. While all stated that global warming was a hoax, the reasons for the hoax ranged from a secret international cabal of the super-rich, to the effects of El Niño and La Niña. One group calmly claimed that the world was actually not warming but cooling and produced spurious scientific research to back up their claims. These groups were mostly ignored by the media crews, as it became clear within a very short space of time that the proponents of the super-rich theory could not explain in any way that was even remotely coherent why the super-rich would be creating the hoax in the first place.

Some proponents of the El Niño and La Niña effects were interviewed as they seemed at first to be a bit more rational. But it also soon became clear that they didn't know what these events actually were and these were just trigger words for their beef against the people they branded as doom-merchants. When presented with a reasonable question, they, to a person, quickly descended into parroting asinine 'scientific' phrases and slogans gleaned from social media group-think sessions. Their reliance on straw-man fallacies, sneering insults and name calling of anyone that questioned them saw reporters quickly abandoning the interviews. The same went for the 'cooling' group.

A well-known conspiracy theorist arrived, one that had legions of followers on social media. An intrepid reporter stood talking to him. She listened, poker-faced, while he spouted his theory that the royal navy had developed an extreme wave-making weapon designed to destroy enemy coastal defences and harbours. He insisted that he had evidence that even the prime minister didn't know about. He also claimed that he had concrete proof that the weapon had been fitted to a submarine and had been used against Wychborough as part of the government's plan to move the population inland to cities, where they could be chipped and tracked more easily.

He handed over a dossier of his 'research', almost begging the reporter to publish the handwritten notes, before 'it was too late'. She took the file and left the man, who was almost in tears. She would give the file to her sister who was doing a

PhD on the growth in popularity of conspiracy theorists and the destructive role that social media was playing.

None of this mattered to the crew of the RV Neptune. Their job was to map the sea floor to ascertain how much this particularly violent storm had changed the underwater topography. Scientists on board were tasked with working out if this might make storm surges worse in the future.

They had completed a scan of the area, reporting that vast amounts of sand had been deposited on the seabed, and that it *would* have a dramatic effect on sea currents unless tidal action dispersed the build-up. A scan of the coastline to the north of the village had shown the seabed to be largely undisturbed, and the next task was to find out where all the sand had come from. The anchor had been winched in, and the vessel made ready to move south by a couple of miles to the area of coast known as Southmere.

The underwater camera operator pointed excitedly at her screen. "I think we know where all the sand has come from."

The crew gathered around the monitor and saw images of buildings looming out of the murky water as the operator guided her camera through the submarine environment. They had all seen submerged buildings before, some in the waters off the coast of Suffolk, but never this far out and never this many.

This area had been surveyed before; the captain called up a chart of the seabed from the last survey, noting that it had taken place just two years previously, and it showed no indication of submerged buildings. He checked the depth of the camera against the depth indicated on the chart, the sea floor here was five metres lower. Many of the buildings were almost intact, with walls still standing, and only the roofs and other wooden parts rotted away. Others stood complete, protected from the currents by layers of sand, sand that was now further up the coast.

A buzz of excitement ran through the crew as they watched the monitor, some counting the buildings as they came into view. All realised that they were part of a discovery, all realised that this would be their moment in history. And all got out their phones and took smiling single and group selfies, ensuring that the monitor displaying the submerged village was visible in the background.

"Thousands of tons of sand have just been sucked up and deposited two miles away, unbelievable," muttered the captain. All were excited, except for the senior ocean scientist on board, his expression was grim. He turned to the captain.

"Yes, the discovery of this sunken village is important, but the reason for its exposure is cause for great worry. As you said, thousands, possibly hundreds of thousands of tons of sand and shingle have been moved over the course of two days. Climate change models have predicted that sea currents around coasts will change and get much stronger. Though what we can't predict is the hydrodynamics that will result from such huge changes. We have already seen that wave action is different at Wychborough, and now we can't tell what parts of the coast will need to be defended."

Only the captain seemed to understand the significance. "Sandbars will shift as these events become more frequent, existing charts will become useless and will need to be constantly updated."

One of the crew members turned, jokily rubbing his finger and thumb together as if holding money. "More work for us."

The scientist glared at him. "I would hardly consider that a benefit of global warming!"

Chapter 2
The News

"…it's not all bad news about the storm so now we go over to our reporter, Suzy Manning, for news of an exciting discovery off the coast of Suffolk." Julia Sutton, the presenter of the east of England news channel, turned to face a giant video screen. The image quickly changed to a feed directly from the reporter.

Suzy Manning was standing on the deck of a ship, feeling particularly unglamourous in the fluorescent orange lifejacket that swamped her tiny frame. The wind had picked up, the sea was choppy, and it was dark. Every couple of seconds, a wave would hit the side of the vessel throwing up a fine spray of freezing salty water. But she stayed professional and did her best to smile through the biting cold and her obvious uncertainty as she tried to maintain her balance on the rolling deck.

Her cameraman indicated that they were broadcasting live. "I'm here on the deck of the research vessel the RV Neptune with the ship's captain. What can you tell us about your discovery, captain?"

"Well, Suzy, as I was telling you earlier, at two thirty this afternoon our underwater camera discovered a previously unmapped submerged village, two miles out."

"You weren't looking for the village though, were you?"

"That is correct. After the storm that washed away so much of the cliff at Wychborough, we were called in to map changes in the seabed. There has been a significant change, and we were looking to see if there were any other areas that had similar changes." The captain paused and seemed to not know what to say next.

Suzy prompted him, "What makes this find so significant is that the village is almost complete."

"Erm, yes, that's right, and although it's quite murky down there, our cameras were able to navigate around the entire village and it's almost as if the whole place was just picked up and dumped in the sea."

"How could you explain that?"

"Well, we've seen how much damage the storm and tidal surge caused in Wychborough. The cliffs around this part of the coast are quite sandy, and it is conceivable that in the past, an even more violent storm was able to do the damage."

"Is the name of the village known?"

"Oh yes, ancient maps say it's the old village of Southmere."

"Thank you, Captain, now back to Julia in the studio."

Three miles further along the coast was the village of Foxmere, where lived the eighty-five-year-old retired Catholic priest, Father O'Sullivan. He turned off the TV and was filled with a deep and troubling sense of foreboding. "It's not Southmere, it's Twinmere."

Back on deck, Suzy tried to remain still while staring into the camera lens until the light went out and she was sure the transmission was over. Only then did she let her anxiety show as she staggered to one side to keep her balance in the roughening sea.

"I had oranges before going on air, because apparently they taste the same coming up as they do going down, which is just as well, because I'm going to throw up now."

She dropped the mic and ran to the gunwale, retching, alarmed as the ship heaved over in the swell and the sea rose up towards her. The ship pitched down and the microphone rolled out of one of the drain holes in the gunwale and down into the sea.

"Well done, Suzy," muttered her cameraman. "That mic only cost a thousand pounds."

The captain took the deathly white reporter by the arm. "You'd better go inside, we've just had another storm warning and it's going to get rough." The cameraman had wasted no time and was already inside, wiping the salt spray off all his equipment.

"Rough! And this isn't rough?" she gasped.

"No, this is quite mild."

Panic started to grip her. "I've got to get off this boat."

"I'm sorry, but it'll be far too dangerous for an inflatable. The storm should pass in a few hours."

"A few hours?" she muttered, anxious at the prospect of being stuck on board the pitching vessel until the storm passed. She clung on to the captain as he led her inside, closing the door just as a huge wave broke over the bow and slammed into the window. She jumped back, frightened.

The captain saw how scared she was and reassured her, "Don't worry, it's reinforced glass, it's actually bulletproof, it won't break. This is nothing compared to what we see in the south Atlantic."

She grabbed the captain's arm as the ship rolled over to an alarming degree. "Become a TV reporter, they said, you'll get sent to all these exotic locations, they said... well, screw this for a lark." She stopped and held her stomach. "Where's the toilet, I'm going to be sick again!"

Six hours later, Suzy was in a stretcher getting soaked by the torrential rain while being helicoptered off the pitching ship, having fallen while rushing to the toilet for yet another dry-heaving session. She'd bumped her head and had been rendered unconscious.

Chapter 3
The Lodge at Southmere

Five Months Later

Nine-year-old Julius looked up at his mother. "Me and Darren want to sleep outside in the tent."

Carol Wilson, Julius' mother, frowned slightly. "Where are your manners, Julius? It's 'Darren and I want to sleep outside', isn't it!" They were on holiday, so she wasn't as firm as she usually was when she corrected him.

"Yes Mum." He shuffled for a bit. "But you didn't say no, so can we?"

"That depends on Darren's mum, doesn't it? Because you're not sleeping outside on your own."

"Darren says his mum said he can."

"Well, I'd better check, because you know what Darren's like, he might be playing a trick on you."

Laura and Darren entered the lodge having heard the conversation. "That's okay, he did ask me, and I did say yes, providing that you agreed."

Carol turned to her son. "Well, in that case, yes, you can sleep outside tonight."

"All night?" asked a hopeful Darren.

"If you want to, then yes." Laura looked at Carol who nodded her agreement.

The Wilsons and the Turners had been neighbours and good friends for years, and this was the first time they'd been on holiday together, despite having talked about it since before their boys were born. Darren Turner was the older of the two boys, older by a week, and he just assumed that this made him the boss, able to dictate what games they played. Julius didn't mind, they played well together, and while Julius was starting to show an interest in science, Darren had a vivid imagination, showing a nascent flair for drama. Julius was happy to play the games that Darren dreamt up, but he was a little bit naïve and tended to believe everything that Darren said.

"We're going to tell each other scary stories, aren't we, Juli!"

"Don't call me Juli, my name's Julius; people will think I'm a girl." Carol was pleased with Julius as for once he had stood up for himself.

"We'll find out if you're a girl when I tell you a scary story tonight," laughed Darren.

Laura wagged her finger at her son. "Don't make it too scary, you need to get a good night's sleep tonight. We're going to spend all day on the beach tomorrow and I don't want you moaning about being too tired."

"I won't, Mum," Darren replied unconvincingly and smirking.

"Promise me, because we all know what you're like," Laura mildly admonished her son, and like Carol was with Julius, she kept it light, the families were on holiday, and no one wanted it to get too serious. "Show me your hands when you say it, so I can see if you've got your fingers crossed."

Darren held out his hands. "I promise, and I didn't have my fingers crossed, but I did have my legs crossed."

"That doesn't count."

He smirked. "Nanna says it does," he replied cheekily.

Julius looked up at his mother. "Do I have to wear my pyjamas?"

"No, you'll get too cold, you can keep your football kit on, but I'll get your trackie bottoms and a hoody to sleep in and you'll have to take your shoes off when you get into the sleeping bag."

"I want to sleep in my kit, I don't care about getting cold," announced Darren.

Laura smiled at her son's bravado. "I'll get your trackie bottoms and hoody anyway."

Just then the husbands arrived from their hour-long round-trip to the nearest convenience store, a trip that should have only taken then twenty minutes. They placed down bulging bags of groceries, most of which comprised of beer.

The two women looked at each other and raised their eyebrows.

"We said to get the essentials!" laughed Carol.

Her husband, Steve, said nothing but slowly lifted out a bottle of Chenin Blanc from the bag.

"Well, obviously, that's an essential!"

"What took you so long?" asked Laura.

Neil, her husband, smirked as he lifted a bottle of Malbec from his bag and showed it to her. "They didn't have any decent wine."

"Well, don't just stand there holding it, pour some out!"

"Steve and I are going to cook tonight," he chuckled proudly as he opened various cupboards looking for wine glasses, failing to see them and getting out teacups instead.

Laura put the teacups away, got out the wine glasses then turned to Carol. "Oh God, Carol, did you bring any indigestion tablets? Christ knows what these two are going to concoct."

Steve frowned with an exaggerated expression of reassurance. "When Neil says 'cook', what he means is we're going to put a couple of pizzas in the oven."

"And you are going to take the wrapping off them first, aren't you? We don't want a repeat of last time," laughed Carol.

Both men feigned hurt, but knew she was right. Last time they tried to cook a pizza, they got drunk, and it was a disaster. Though Laura's social media post of the melted plastic on the burned pizza did get over a thousand likes and fifty shares.

The holiday lodge was a two-story wooden structure situated in the wood close to the cliffs on the Suffolk coast, and despite the area being listed as Southmere village, there was no village, only the wood. The lodge was a new build, it had been designed to resemble an old alpine ski lodge and they were its first occupants—something that pleased the women as everything was new, clean and smelled fresh; the men didn't even notice. There were a couple of other properties in the wood, but they were a fair distance away and unoccupied. All in all, the lodge was private enough without being remote. The adults each grabbed their favourite alcoholic drink and went to stand on the veranda.

Carol sighed and looked wistfully into the distance, putting her hand to her ear. "Listen to that, just listen."

Steve cocked his head. "Listen to what? I can't hear anything."

"Exactly, no cars, no planes, no dogs barking and their owners yelling at them, just the sound of the leaves in the trees and the waves on the beach below us."

"Well, that was hopelessly romantic," muttered Steve as he tried and failed to supress a burp.

They all laughed at his embarrassment, then watched the boys struggling to put together the EEZEE-UP tent that they had brought.

Laura looked out over the heathland then went inside and got the powerful and expensive binoculars that her husband had purchased for birdwatching, even though he had previously shown no interest in birdwatching. She scanned the area, stopping at one point, then moved from side to side to check out the rest of the heath. She pointed to a patch of gorse in the distance where the growth was stunted. The area was vaguely circular and appeared to be about twenty metres across. Some birds were flying towards it, then suddenly changed direction and flew around the periphery. She handed the binoculars to her husband.

"What do you think might have happened there?"

He focussed on the area. "Dunno," he grunted, before handing them back.

She zoomed in to the affected area. "Hardly anything is growing in that middle bit, certainly no flowers, just scrubby ferns and whatever those other plants are," she muttered as she studied the area again. Then she looked at the heathland surrounding the stunted area. "I can see rabbits scampering around outside of the patch, but none inside, they seem to be avoiding it too. Weird."

Steve pointed to the area. "Animals know things; it's thought that as human intelligence developed, we lost a sixth sense, but animals still have it, like when a dog can sense danger and they suddenly jump up and bark to warn their owners."

Carol looked at Laura and rolled her eyes comedically.

Neil frowned, trying to concentrate as the beer started to take effect. "I read a bit about this area; back in the middle ages Southmere was an important village. There was a copper works, and trees were cut down to be made into charcoal, maybe that's where some trees were." It was a feeble attempt at an explanation, and he knew it. "Apparently, the copper they produced was superior quality," he quickly added, trying to redeem himself.

He took the binoculars and studied the area. "I'd say it's about a kilometre away, maybe a bit more. There was a bit about the village on TV a while back. It was lost to the sea as the cliffs crumbled, apparently it's about two K's out under the sea and it's still in roughly the same layout as it was back then." He scanned across the patch, noticing that what little vegetation was there seemed to get even thinner as it got close to the centre. "I reckon that's where they dumped toxic waste products, they weren't very environmentally aware back then and would have just wanted it far away from the village."

Steve took the binoculars and zoomed into the area. "Yeah," he grunted through another beer burp. "The animals must sense that there's danger there. They can't possibly know why, but they just know to stay away."

Neil took the binoculars back, and he too scanned the area. Laura looked at Carol and raised her eyebrows. "Oh God, what have I started?" she whispered. Neil and Steve didn't hear her.

"They're going to spend the rest of the day discussing science," whispered Carol.

"They damn well better not, we have requirements that they need to tend to, don't we!" Laura huffed, feigning indignance.

"Too right they do!"

Neil handed the binoculars back. "By-products of copper are very toxic, the people would have known that and would have wanted it far away from a water source. Perhaps the ground there is still a bit polluted. We better not go in there."

Laura looked at her husband with an amused frown. "What on earth would we want to go into the heath for? We're going to the beach to get some sun this week, aren't we, Carol."

"Too bloody right we are, I didn't buy a new bikini to swim in the sea, it's too damn cold."

The four dismissed their speculation about the stunted growth as Steve got some more drinks. They drank while chuckling at the boys' efforts with the tent.

Carol turned to her husband as her mothering instinct kicked back in. "The boys will be alright out here tonight, won't they?"

Steve pointed up to a floodlight and CCTV camera. "They'll be fine. But if you're worried about them, you can stay up all night watching them on the monitor."

She shoved him playfully. "Oh shush, you know what I'm like."

"Well, you did say that Julius needs to start standing up for himself, and staying outside tonight will be good for his confidence."

She looked up at the camera and felt reassured. "Yeah, that's true."

Neil finished his beer and went to get another. Laura stroked his arm affectionately and looked into his eyes. "Don't have too much to drink, because we *are* on holiday, aren't we?"

Carol eased a fresh bottle from Steve's hand before he could open it. "Good point. Performance is required tonight."

Laura frowned. "No, Carol. Performance is demanded!"

Both women stood with their hands on their hips. "You men better be up to it."

"Oh we will, don't you worry about that."

The tent was finally up, both boys were playing inside, oblivious to their parents' suggestive comments.

Pizzas cooked and eaten, the adults settled down to unwind from their jobs and had a half-hearted discussion of what they wanted to do in the next seven days. The boys had chucked their sleeping bags in the tent and were playing outside building a den out of sticks that they found.

It started to get dark, the mothers went to the tent and prepared sleeping bags and torches, with Carol handing over Julius' old toy walkie-talkie that had an alarm buzzer on it.

"If you get scared and need me, just press this button, and the door will be open if you need to come in to go to the toilet.

There are bottles of water and some torches, and the outside light will be on. Okay, Julius?"

Julius blushed at his mother's fussing and was bothered that he might get a ribbing from Darren about it. "I am nine, Mum, I'm not a baby anymore." He was trying to be brave, but he had never slept outside before and was starting to look a little nervous. Darren had spotted how worried Julius seemed to be getting and knew he had a good story to frighten him with.

With the boys outside, the adults chatted, with each one wishing the time away until they could get to the point where they could go to their rooms. Each one of the adults did that thing as the time approached ten o'clock, they all were trying to bring conversation to a close, and all knew why they were doing it. Steve eventually stretched and forced a yawn, then smirked.

"I don't know about you lot, but I'm ready for bed."

Laura laughed then winked at Carol. "I think we're all ready for bed."

Carol stood up. "Laura and I will just go and check on the boys, why don't you have a shower, Steve?"

"I was intending to."

"So was I, I like to be nice and clean when I get in bed," grinned Neil.

"We'll have showers when we come back in. Don't worry, we won't be long."

The two women went outside. "I don't mind admitting that what with both of us working I've had a bit of a dry spell, and it's gone on for a bit too long," grumbled Carol.

Laura nodded knowingly. "Yeah, me too. Darren's quite active now and getting him to bed at a sensible time is difficult, and by the time he's stopped making any noise and is asleep, we're both too tired. Plus, he does have this habit of waking up, he's knocked on the bedroom door a couple of times, and that is always at the back of my mind and it always puts the brakes on the er, let's call them the proceedings. So them being outside tonight is perfect." She smirked, slightly embarrassed. "And to be honest, I can only really let go when we're on holiday."

Carol frowned. "Yeah me too. When it's at home, my head is always full of all the crappy mundane things, shopping, washing, ironing, you know what it's like."

Laura nodded frustratedly. "Oh yes, I know that feeling all too well."

Carol blushed then giggled a bit. "I shouldn't really say this, but it's been a couple of months now, and last time when we were, you know, doing it, halfway through I looked up and noticed a cobweb, then I started thinking about how long it had been since I did the dusting!"

Laura stifled a laugh, then blushed. "Don't feel bad, it's been a while for us too and the last time we were at it, halfway through I suddenly remembered that I hadn't paid a credit card bill. I looked at the clock and it was quarter to twelve, so I erm..." She wiggled her index finger around a bit. "...so I did this thing that always hurries him along so I could get my phone and make a payment before midnight, because I was worried that we'd get a late payment charge. How bad was that?"

Carol laughed. "I don't feel so bad now."

Laura turned and looked back into the lodge.

"Neil better not have had too much to drink, because..." She crossed her legs and squeezed her thighs together. "I'm, you know, feeling a bit fruity."

Carol smirked then looked up and down at Laura. "Even if he has, with your body, I'm sure you can think of ways to get him interested." She blushed again. "I do this thing for Steve that always gets him going."

"Ooh, do tell."

"I'll tell you tomorrow, I have to see if it still works, 'cos like I said, it's been a while." She thought for a bit, then smirked. "Yeah, I'll make it work."

The boys were fine, to the point of ignoring their mothers, and the two women went back in to find that both men were showered and in their bedrooms.

Laura chuckled. "I think they're quite keen, don't you?"

"It's nice to have an én-suite in all the bedrooms, isn't it? I think we'll have one fitted at home."

Chapter 4
Storytime

"…and they were never seen again." Julius sat back, proud of the story he had come up with. Darren looked at him, then burst out laughing.

"That was rubbish. A ten-foot tall spider? that was just silly, they don't exist."

Julius pouted. "It did in my story."

"Okay." Darren pulled himself up straight, a naughty grin on his face. "Well, it's my turn to tell a story, but the monster in this one *is* real." His eyes sparkled as he saw Julius cringe slightly.

Darren looked all around pretending to be nervous, then lowered his voice.

"There's a monster that lives in the ground near here, my nanna said we shouldn't have come here. She said that when she was a little girl, her nanna told her of a monster, and no one must ever say its name," he whispered ominously.

Julius' eyes opened wide. "What happens if you say its name?"

"It comes and gets you, and you're never seen alive again, only your skeleton is found."

He saw the look of fear in Julius's eyes and decided to embellish the story to have a bit of fun at his friend's expense. "It's a horrible looking monster and the first thing it does is to use one of its claws to scoop out one of your eyeballs and eat it; it leaves the other one in, so you'll be able to see as it chews on your legs. It keeps you alive for as long as possible, but you can't get away because it's pinning you down with one of its claws through here."

He poked a terrified Julius in the stomach, making him jump back. "And all the time you're screaming in pain, knowing that there's nothing you can do and you're going to die in agony. Its tongue is raspy, like a cat's, only much rougher, with one lick it can scrape all the muscle away from bone. Then it eats your guts, and you die."

"Do you know what its name is?" whimpered Julius.

"Yeah. I worked it out. I found this old book, it was at my nanna's, and it's old, well older than her, it's like, really, really old. In it is a series of numbers and I'd read about codes using numbers, you know, A equals one, B equals two, yeah? So I guessed that the numbers were the code to its name. I wrote them down."

He pulled a bit of paper from his pocket and laid it out, on it were numbers.

20, 8, 5, 20, 23, 9, 14, 13, 5, 18, 5, 2, 5, 1, 19, 20.

"Using the code, it says…"

Julius held his hands up. "No, Darren, stop! Remember what your nanna said, no one must mention its name."

"My nanna's a bit loopy, so she probably made it all up."

"But what about the code? Someone must have written it for a reason."

Darren waved him away. "The Twinmere Beast. There! I've said it."

"Ooh, did you feel that?" Carol shivered as she dropped the dressing gown on the floor. "A chill ran right down my spine, and I've gone all cold."

"Yeah, I felt it too, there must be a draft in here, and I'm not surprised you felt the cold, as you don't actually have any clothes on, do you. But you know, get in bed and we'll soon find a way to get warm."

He looked her up and down, admiring her trim figure that even after childbirth, hadn't changed since they first met all those years ago when she was eighteen and he was twenty. Without realising it, he let out the same lustful sigh that he'd done the first time he saw her naked.

She grinned lasciviously as she slowly walked towards him, pleased that he was looking at her; she looked up and down at him and was even more pleased that after being together for seventeen years he was still aroused at the sight of her naked body.

"Oh no!" gasped Father O'Sullivan as he sat bolt upright in bed and shivered, a cold sweat forming on his brow. "Please God, no. Don't let this happen." This was the moment he had been dreading for the past five months. Since the discovery of the lost village, his fear was that someone would say the beast's name, and if the old name for the village became common knowledge, then more would say the name and there would be no stopping the beast.

Out in the tent, a shivering, terrified Julius sat open-mouthed in shock. "What have you done? What if it's real?"

"Maybe it is, maybe it isn't, but I told you my nanna's a bit odd."

"But what about the numbers?"

"I dunno, do I? maybe someone was playing a prank, they did have jokes back then."

In the heath, in the middle of the area of stunted undergrowth, a fine mist rose up out of the ground and started to drift towards the lodge. At first, no foliage was disturbed as the vapour flowed around the plants, but gradually a solid began to take form. First the eyes, then the body, and by the time it was out of the heath and onto solid ground it was fully formed like a man on his hands and knees. Long claws sat at the end of long bony fingers, its jaw hung open showing row upon row of jagged teeth. Its skin was scaley and iridescent, catching the moonlight and reflecting it with purple, blue and green hues.

It moved silently and slowly, but inexorably towards the lodge. Soon it was at the edge of the wood, it's unblinking eyes focussed on the tent. The floodlight was on the other side of the tent and the beast was in its shadow. Had the boys looked around they would have seen it slowly crawling towards them, illuminated by the dappled moonlight filtering down through the trees.

"Why did you have to tell me about the beast? Why did you have to say its name? I'm a bit scared now."

"Well, you might be scared, but it doesn't frighten me, I've got this." Darren produced his father's penknife. "Dad thought he'd lost it, but I found it, it's well sharp, look." He picked up a small branch about the thickness of his little finger. One slash was all it took to cut clean through the wood. "When the beast gets here, I'll stab it, I'll slash it, I'll use it's blood as war paint, then I'll gouge it's eyes out, I'll slit open its belly and pull its guts out and wear them as a scarf."

Julius sat back in horror, Darren could see how frightened he was.

"Don't worry, Juli, it won't want you, because I said its name, and anyway, you're too skinny, but I'll protect you, after all, I am the oldest. If the beast grabs you first, I'll cut its arms off before it has a chance to eat you alive." Darren sat back laughing at his friend.

"Shut up, Darren, I don't like it. Do you think the beast is real?"

"Yeah." Darren lunged at Julius with his hands up like claws and his mouth open, baring his teeth, making Julius jump back.

"Stop it, I'm frightened."

"Well, if you're scared, we can go into the tent. My other nanna says what you can't see can't hurt you."

"I think it can," mumbled Julius as the two boys got in the tent. "Just because you can't see something, it doesn't mean it isn't there."

Darren held a torch under his chin and turned it on, making Julius jump again.

"I'm going in."

"Okay, Juli, I knew you'd be a girl. I'll stay out here while you go to your mummy." He waved the penknife around as if in a swordfight. "I'm not afraid of the beast."

"Oh God, oh God, oh God," gasped Carol. She closed her mouth and held her breath, her face going red as the climax built inside her.

"I'm going to…" panted Steve as sweat trickled down his spine. Both were on the point of orgasm when the walkie-talkie beeped.

"Oh I don't believe it," grunted Steve as he rolled off his wife. "Couldn't he have waited another ten seconds!" Carol glared at the walkie-talkie. "Another twenty seconds would have been better," she grumbled, then reluctantly picked up the handset. Her mothering instinct overrode her lustful desires, but she still found it hard to hide her disappointment. "What is it, Julius!"

"I'm scared."

"You said you wanted to stay outside tonight!" she snapped.

"But I'm frightened, can I come in?"

Carol looked at Steve, they both burst out laughing. "Oh go on, Julius, you can come in."

She turned back to her husband. "We'd better let Laura and Neil know, they won't want Darren out there on his own."

Steve shook his head. "I'm not knocking on their door, because..." He cocked his ear and heard the faint grunting and rhythmic squeaking of a bed. "...I can hear them at it."

"I'll go," grumbled a frustrated Carol as she pulled on a dressing gown.

She felt awkward and she stood outside the door and could hear their friend's activity and Laura's gasping, she hesitated for a moment but couldn't wait any longer. She knocked on their door. "Sorry guys, but Julius is frightened and has come in, shall I go and get Darren?"

She heard a grunt from Neil and a few moments later, the door was opened a fraction by an obviously naked Laura. "Darren will be fine outside."

Carol bit the side of her lip and cringed slightly. "Were you..."

"Yep, right on the point."

"So was I, sorry. I'll send Julius back out." Embarrassed, Carol went downstairs to find a sheepish looking Julius standing in the kitchen.

"What were you frightened by?" she demanded, her disappointment making the words come out a bit firmer than she intended.

"Darren told me a scary story about a monster," he whimpered. Frustration had got the better of her and Carol found herself getting annoyed rather than being sympathetic.

"Well, that's all it was, a story! Now, you said you're a big boy and that you wanted to sleep outside. So if you are a big boy, you have to be brave, so you go back out there, Darren is out there on his own; go and keep him company, and only call me if it's a real emergency. A story about a monster isn't an emergency! Now off you go."

Inside the tent, Darren was chuckling to himself and fiddling with the knife, opening it and closing it, unaware that just the other side of the nylon, the beast was making ready to take him. He didn't hear the needle point of the claw silently pierce the light fabric. He didn't hear the material being slit open as the razor-sharp inner edge of the claw was drawn down, effortlessly slicing through the fabric. He wasn't aware of the beast's hands that were reaching in to grab him.

With its hand over Darren's mouth to silence him and its arm around his body, the beast turned to leave, briefly stepping into the bright white light of the security floodlight. It flinched, quickly drawing the limb away as the light burned and a couple of the scales hardened and dropped off.

Julius went back outside, and Carol went back to the bedroom. She took off her dressing gown and got on top of her husband. "Let's continue where we left off, shall we?"

Julius got to the tent to find it slit open and empty, the open penknife in the tent and the torch laying on the ground outside.

"Darren?" he called out nervously. "Darren, where are you?" There was no reply. "Darren! Darren! Come on, Darren, this isn't funny."

He remembered his mother's words about being brave and picked up the torch, shining it into the trees and bushes, but afraid of what he might see, and afraid that Darren might jump out at him.

"Come on, Darren, stop hiding, it really isn't funny," he shouted, raising his voice to cover his fear. He took a couple of tentative steps forward, summoning all his courage as he stepped into the shadow of the tent.

In the bedroom, Carol was rising to an orgasm again, panting and tugging at the sheet.

"Oh God," she gasped. "I'm going to..." She held her breath as her back arched.

Realising that this was serious, Julius went back to the tent and pressed the button on the walkie-talkie.

The beeper sounded. "I don't fucking believe it," she shouted. Steve sighed and rolled off her as she snatched up the radio. She turned to Steve. "We're not going to do anything else tonight, so why don't you finish yourself off while I deal with Julius." She pressed the answer button. "I told you to only use the radio if it's an emergency, I said that Darren telling you a scary story is not an emergency," she snapped.

"Mum, Darren isn't here."

"What!"

"He's not in the tent. I've looked all around for him."

"Well, where is he then?" she demanded.

"I don't know. I can't find him."

Carol picked up her dressing gown, frowning.

"What's up?" grunted Steve.

"Julius says that Darren isn't in the tent, and he doesn't know where he is."

Steve's face dropped. "Oh, that could be serious."

"This better be one of Darren's pranks and *not* anything serious. I'm going to have a look," she muttered.

Steve rolled out of bed and pulled on his boxers. "I'm coming with you."

The two got downstairs to find a terrified Julius in the kitchen, shaking and near to tears. Carol's irritation instantly disappeared as she saw how frightened he was and became concerned as she was hit with the fear that this really could be serious. She put her arms around him as he started to cry.

"I don't know where he is… he was in the tent when I came in before… but he's not there now," he managed to say between sobs.

"Don't worry, Julius, he's probably just hiding to play a trick on you, he knows how easily scared you are." She tried to hide the fear that all parents have and hoped that Julius hadn't picked up on it.

Steve's disappointment immediately subsided as he saw the fear in his son's eyes.

Both parents took him by the hand as they went outside. Five minutes later, and with anxiety rising, they still hadn't found Darren.

They didn't hear the scream in the distance, the mercifully short scream.

Carol was unable to hide the worry that she felt. "I'm going to get Laura and Neil." She ran upstairs, not waiting to knock and burst into their bedroom. "Darren's missing!"

Neil and Laura looked in through the slit in the side of the tent and the first things she saw were the tracksuit bottoms and hoody still folded where she left them. The first thing Neil saw was his penknife open and lying on the ground.

"That's my knife, I thought I'd lost it, but Darren must have taken it."

"He knows how cross you get when you see him playing with knives. He's cut the fabric and is hiding, he must think you're going to tell him off," muttered Laura quietly, desperate to come up with a rational answer to avoid the reason that they were all thinking—that someone had kidnapped Darren.

"I promise I won't be cross with you," shouted Neil, trying to sound firm but conciliatory, though unable to cover the shake in his voice as he too was just trying to find logical reason for the boys' disappearance. "Come out from wherever you are hiding, and we'll all go inside."

After another five minutes of fruitless searching, Steve suddenly pointed back to the house. "The CCTV! That should tell us what happened. You carry on searching, I'll go and have a look."

He went in to look for the recorder, leaving Laura, Neil and Carol calling Darren's name, all three of them with rising panic. Carol held a crying Julius tight. Eventually Steve located the recorder in a cupboard under the stairs. He selected the frame that showed the area where the tent was, but only a small part of the tent was visible in the top left corner of the frame. The light from the powerful halogen bulb had a sharp cut-off edge and only a tiny bit of the tent was illuminated. He kicked himself for not checking the camera feed before, if he had done that he would have seen that the tent was almost out of shot and he could have adjusted the angle of the camera and the floodlight. But he hadn't, and with shaking hands he rewound until he saw Julius walking towards the house for the first time.

"He said Darren was in the tent when he came in, but he wasn't there when Carol sent him back out," he muttered under his breath. He pressed 'Play' and after a little while, he thought he saw the tent twitch slightly and a movement by the side, it was brief and he couldn't make out what it was. Even though the air had been quite still all night, he convinced himself that there must have been a gust and it was the tent flapping in the light breeze. He continued to watch until he saw Julius appear and start looking for Darren. He stopped the playback when he saw his distressed son making his way back to the lodge.

He went back out. "There's nothing on the CCTV."

Laura was beside herself with worry, Neil's expression was concern mixed with anger, Carol was near to tears. Steve realised that he was going to have to be the one to say it.

"We have to call the police."

The wind had got up while they had been out and the light rustling of the leaves in the trees created a creepy atmosphere, adding to the tension and driving the distraught Laura to tears. If any of them had looked behind, they would have seen the piece of paper with the code being blown away, carried through the wood by the offshore breeze towards the cliff edge and settling in the branches of a gorse bush. But they didn't look behind, and nobody saw the two small, vaguely triangular shapes on the ground mixed in with the leaves.

Chapter 5
The Search

The police helicopter flew in ever widening circles above the wood, its searchlight scanning the ground, the roar of its engine and the beat of its rotor blades sending a chill through both sets of parents. Blue lights flashed and teams of officers searched through the wood, their powerful torches creating hard sinister shadows. In the lodge, officers were trying to take a statement from the near hysterical Laura. Neil was trying to comfort her as she described the football kit that Darren was wearing. Carol and Steve had made their statements and were sitting, hugging their son, staring into space, all three numb from the shock.

A specialist officer had tried to get a statement from Julius and was shaking her head. She went to the detective sergeant Griffin who was in charge and who as studying the CCTV recording.

"All that he will say is that Darren said something he shouldn't have. But he won't say what it is, he says it's dangerous."

"What do you think?"

"The kid's in shock. His parents say that he'd come in frightened, saying that Darren had told him a story about a monster. His mother sent him back out and Darren wasn't there. He'll need to see a child psychologist, I doubt we'll ever get anything from him."

The detective pointed to the CCTV screen. "Carol Wilson estimates the time between Julius coming in and her sending him back out to be less than five minutes, and the CCTV recording confirms that. Though there's something on this recording during the time Julius was in the lodge, but it's too dark. I'll see if I can get it improved."

The helicopter had circled over the edge of the cliff for the second time, once again shining its spotlight down onto the beach. The downdraught dislodged the paper which fluttered down to the shingle below, getting stuck in a tuft of long grass close to the cliff face.

The scene was tapped off; Julius and both sets of parents were taken to the station as the search continued. Griffin downloaded the video to a USB stick and went out to the officer in charge of the search team.

"There may be something on this video, and the sooner we know what it is the better, so I have to get back to the station to get it enhanced, you carry on here."

Chapter 6
The Scale

Griffin peered at the unenhanced image from the CCTV. The playback on the recorder in the lodge had no image adjustment controls, just rewind and play. This machine was far more powerful. There was definitely a movement, the fabric of the tent rippled, and something briefly appeared beside the tent, though even with the raw file it was clearly not the boy. It was frustrating that only the lower quarter of the tent was visible, but adjustment of contrast and brightness should change that.

A few minutes of tweaking by the technician brought the image to be as good as it was ever going to get. Despite the powerful white of the floodlight, adjusting colour, saturation and hue was not possible as this camera was in night mode as the camera's timer had switched it to infrared. There was enough IR from the floodlight for it to work, but the image was greyscale. Though it was a new, modern camera and the image was sharp.

"Is that a leg?" muttered the technician as he stepped back and forth through the images. "It doesn't look like a human leg, but it's too big for an animal, at least not a muntjac deer, they're the only ones in this part of the country and there haven't been any seen in the Southmere wood for years."

"Can you zoom in on it?"

"Yeah."

The technician selected an area around what they thought was a leg and selected 'X2'. The double-size image wasn't that much help.

"Go bigger."

"If I go any bigger then we'll lose definition."

"Do it anyway."

At 'X5', the image was far too pixelated, so they stepped back to the previous setting.

"It's less than a second, create a loop and run it in slow-motion."

They studied the image as it repeated over and over. The object moved into the light but was suddenly snatched away.

"Whatever that thing is, it looks like it was pulled away as if it was hurt. Step through one frame at a time."

The technician rewound a few seconds then tapped the spacebar to advance the video.

"What are you looking for?"

"I won't know until I see it." Even at twenty-five frames per second, the image was blurred by the rapid movement, but a couple of frames seemed to show a wisp of something.

"Stop! Does that look like steam or smoke to you?"

"Yes, and it looks like something's fallen off whatever that thing is."

"We need to find it."

Chapter 7
Father O'Sullivan

Unable to get back to sleep, Father O'Sullivan got out of bed, pulled on a dressing gown, went downstairs and made his way to his library. He got a set of steps and went to the top-most shelf and reached up to an ancient book.

"What are you doing up there, Father?" came the gentle admonishing voice of Orla O'Dowd, his housekeeper for the past sixty-five years. "Will you look at the time, it's gone midnight! Now you get yourself down from there or you'll fall. And you haven't got your slippers on, the floor's cold and you'll catch your death."

He ignored her and took the book, then carefully stepped down. He turned to her and she saw the shocked look on his face.

"What is it, Father? What's wrong? I've never seen you like this."

He said nothing and handed her a Bible, then sighed deeply. "You will need this more than ever now."

She looked into his eyes; behind the concern, there was another look. She'd been with him in the seventies when he was a Catholic priest in northern Ireland, and even at the height of the troubles she'd never seen this look. She knew how strong he had been, but now he was afraid of something. He sensed her concern.

"I am afraid, but I am not afraid for myself, and I have never been, my faith has seen to that. But I am afraid of what might happen to others now."

She guided him to a chair where he sat breathing deeply and even deeper in thought. He picked up a small wooden cross and nervously fiddled with it.

"What is it, Father?" she whispered as she anxiously rolled her rosary though her fingers.

He closed his eyes as he thought of the horror that had been released. "Someone has called the beast."

Cold ran through her veins at the realisation of what he'd said. She had heard the stories from an old woman when the pair of them first moved to Foxmere in the early nineties; the ancient legend of the Southmere monster that stalked the land and took whoever said its name. Knowing that legends often have a grain of truth to them, at first, it had frightened her. But the older she got, the more she had pushed it to the back of her mind, dismissing it as a grim fairy tale that was told to children to make them behave.

"Surely it can't be true, Father?"

"I am sorry, Orla, but it is. I felt the beast wake."

She swallowed hard, subconsciously holding the Bible to her heart. "I was suddenly cold, it woke me. So I must have felt it too."

"All references to its name were removed centuries ago, but someone must have known it. May God have mercy on the soul of whoever spoke its name. Let us pray for them."

Orla got on her knees while the father remained sitting in his chair. Both clasped their hands together, praying silently for five minutes.

After they finished, he opened the two-hundred-year-old book. "This is the last publicly available account of a sighting. In fourteen eighty, the beast appeared and took the life of the village blacksmith. A young woman named Rose Fletcher was out fetching a pail of water that night, she claimed to have seen the beast. She was immediately accused of being a witch." He saw Orla flinch.

"Because she was thought to be a witch, she was put to the question." He abruptly stopped and hung his head. "We have to admit, Orla, that the church we love so dearly has done many truly terrible things in the past. This is an account of her ordeal." He opened the book to a specific chapter and turned it to show the yellowing pages.

Orla gasped; she knew exactly what being 'put to the question' meant. Everyone knew what being put to the question meant; it was the inquisition, it was torture. But it was all in the past, though now she feared she was going to read the account of a real person's suffering.

Father O'Sullivan sighed. "The account was written by a junior priest, the assistant to the investigator appointed by the bishop to interrogate all those accused of witchcraft. His job was to record everything."

Many times, the investigator told Rose Fletcher to admit to being a witch, as how else would the beast have passed her by. Many times, she denied being a witch. She was taken to the dungeon. The executioner showed her the many instruments of torture and where upon her body they would be used, but she still refused to admit her guilt. The investigator then declared that it was the devil that was causing her stubbornness and instructed that she be placed in irons and fixed to a wall in a most uncomfortable position. The executioner watched for her to summon her familiars and soon a rat did appear, sent by the devil at her request to comfort her.

The next morning, Rose Fletcher was in a most distressed state, she was given water of the most foul kind but nothing to eat. She was again told to confess to being in league with Satan, to which she denied. Again she was shown the instruments and again she refused to confess and begged the investigator to believe her. Instead, the investigator instructed the executioner to commence the torture. Her hands were tied before her so she could see the screws being placed upon her thumbs. The wretched girl begged to be released but would not confess.

Five times she did shriek as ever more force was applied to crush her fingers. God, being all merciful, caused the girl to pass out to relieve her suffering. She was placed back in the cell and left until the next day.

Upon seeing the rack, the girl fainted, cold water was thrown over her and she awoke to find herself stripped of all her clothes and fixed on the rack, upon which she began the most dreadful wailing. The ropes tightened and the investigator begged her to confess, but still she refused. Many times she did faint, many times she was brought back with cold water. Hot metal was placed upon her skin, she screamed every time, and in the most dreadful way, but still she refused to confess. The investigator stated that it was the devil giving her the strength to endure the great pains that she was suffering and instructed more force to be applied.

Orla skipped over the more detailed accounts of Rose's torture, finding them too distressing, but gasped in horror as she read the final account.

Only when her knees did separate and her arms were pulled from their sockets did she let out one final shriek and said she would confess.
She was placed back in her cell to recover enough to make her confession. She later admitted all the charges against her: that she was a witch, that she did have carnal knowledge of Satan, and that she did direct the beast to the blacksmith. The investigator asked her to describe the beast and instructed me to record everything that was said.
"It rose up out of the ground like a mist, slowly it drifted towards the village, its body taking form, it was like a man on his hands and knees. It turned and looked at me, but it didn't seem interested in me."
"Because you, being a witch, caused it to have no interest in you?"
"Yes."
"Did you direct it to the blacksmith's dwelling?"
"Yes."
"Did it have a tail?"
"No."
"Go on."
"By the time it was at the blacksmith's home, it was fully formed, its skin scaly, its hands had long claws, its mouth opened to show fangs. I didn't see what happened to the

blacksmith, but as the beast returned, its body seemed to be fading back to a mist, eventually it disappeared into the ground."

The next day, she was unable to walk to the gallows to be hanged and had to be carried. She seemed resigned to her fate and did not protest. Her body was so damaged from being put the question that death was a release for her.

Orla wiped the tears from her eyes. "Is that really what we used to do?"

"Yes, it is."

"She only confessed to end her suffering, and probably only held out because she knew she would be hanged if she did."

"Undoubtedly so, and we cannot, we *must not*, deny these things ever happened. But we also have to remember that this was the late fifteenth century, and these were different times, people were ignorant and superstitious. The witch craze had yet to start, but the Malleus Maleficarum had been published and witchery was believed to be real, there was fear, and fear makes people do terrible things."

"How old was she?" Orla's voice was shaky, and she wasn't quite sure if she wanted to know.

He shook his head and sighed. "She was sixteen. I didn't want you to read this to upset you, but her description of the beast matches every other description that had been recorded. The investigator had been sent by the bishop, his primary job was to gain the confessions of witches, but he was also charged with gathering information on the beast. The bishop had compiled a list of previous sightings; all had the same account—vapour rising from the ground and gradually taking the form of a man on his hands and knees."

"This was before the reformation and the Catholic church still held great power in the land. Saying the name of the village was never a problem, it was only when someone said the name and followed it with 'beast' that the beast would be called and the person taken. So the church ordered the name of the village to be changed to Southmere, all documents that referenced Twinmere were altered, and all existing maps destroyed. But shortly after the destruction of the maps there was a series of storms the like of which had never been seen before. In a matter of days a stretch of coastline, ten miles wide and four miles deep was washed into the sea, taking the entire village with it. All of the inhabitants died, the first of which was the investigator."

"Father, that sounds a lot like revenge to me."

"Yes. I have seen church records from the time, there was a bishop's conference, and all agreed that it was the beast's revenge. The report only survived because the young priest left the village before it was renamed. Those who spoke the former name were harshly punished and soon the old name was forgotten."

Orla became anxious. "Father, have there been any incidents since that one?"

"Yes, in 1880, a man went missing and no one knows how he was able to summon the beast. His wife described the beast to the police but was not believed. She was accused of his murder, tried, found guilty and sentenced to death, but because of her ranting about the beast, she was declared insane and placed in an asylum."

He paused, wondering if he should say any more, but Orla had been his constant companion for over sixty years and he felt that she had the right to know.

"A bishop visited her on many occasions, he knew that she was completely sane and told the asylum authorities that it was pastoral care and to give her comfort in her madness, as it was referred to back then. He would hear her confession, but what he was really doing was questioning her about the beast. The woman's description was exactly the same as all the others."

"Does the government know about this?"

"No, they can never know. Governments are run by politicians who get their information from technocrats. None of these people have the capacity to even contemplate the supernatural. If they were informed, and if they believed it, they would want to do research, they would investigate. They would dig up the past and discover the original name of the village and the beast would be free again. No," he said firmly, "the only way to ensure safety is for all the information to stay forever in the church. We can only pray that this is a fluke, a one-off."

But there was one map that had been missed.

Orla glanced up at the clock. "I know it's late, but the bishop needs to know."

"You're right, Orla, I must waste no time. I will call him now."

"You are right to be anxious," said the bishop gravely as Father O'Sullivan finished relating everything he knew about the discovery of the village and the report of its old name. The bishop could not hide his concern. "This is truly worrying. Should the beast get free, then no one will be safe. I shall immediately inform the Cardinal."

Father O'Sullivan's voice was timorous with anxiety. "Your excellency, people must be warned, but how should I do it?"

"You must do what your heart tells you to do, but you must be careful, only the ordained in the Catholic church have the discipline to refrain from saying the beast's name, the ordinary people do not. Even the most devout in the congregation would not be able to resist the temptation. Pray, and the Lord will guide you."

"Thank you for giving this old man your time, your excellency."

"You still have time to do what is right before the Lord calls you."

Father O'Sullivan ended the call; speaking to the bishop had only served to heighten his fears, and he was unable to shake off the restless feeling inside. Little did he know that just a few miles away, not only had the beast been called but had already claimed its first victim in over a century.

It was six-thirty, the sun had just broken over the horizon and after just three hours of sleep, detective Griffin was back at the lodge with the rest of the search team. They had completed the search of the wood the previous night and were on the beach. Griffin stayed at the lodge scanning the area around the tent for whatever it was that appeared to fall off whatever it was in the video. In amongst the twigs and leaf litter, he found what he at first thought was a leaf. It was a rounded triangle about fifty millimetres on either side. It was thin and stiff, dried out like the other detritus on the ground, but it didn't match any of the leaves on the trees. A little bit more searching yielded another one, and both of them seemed to be scorched.

He placed both in an evidence bag, then studied them, trying to work out what they were and if they came from whatever it was that he saw on the CCTV recording.

Chapter 8
The Beating

Arthur Pennock left the corner shop, his shoulders hunched and with a concerned look on his face. He was a worried man, and with very good reason. He had kept a low profile since moving to the area five years previously, keeping himself to himself, not socialising and making no effort to find friends in the village. His home was a remote bungalow about two miles outside the village of Westmere on the Suffolk coast, itself about two miles northwest of Southmere.

The vast majority of his needs were provided online, whether it be shopping or services, and this suited his hermit-like lifestyle. He didn't go out much, he didn't need to, and more importantly, he didn't want to. But every now and then he would run out of something. He didn't have a car and would have to make the long walk to the convenience store in Westmere.

Until last night, the only regular visitors to enter his home had been social workers. But late last night the police had visited him, they had stayed for an hour, and someone had noticed. The police checked his answers to their questions and were satisfied that he was telling the truth. But the police being satisfied didn't count for anything now and he knew it.

He'd hung his head as he paid for the bottle of washing up liquid, but he knew he was getting the look; the revulsion, the sneering distain, the look of disgust he got from people who either knew or guessed at his former life. A couple of years after moving to the area he had been recognised. He had tried to play it down, claiming that it was mistaken identity, and most people believed him, but some were suspicious.

He thought it had all gone away, given his years of self-imposed isolation, and that maybe people would have forgotten and maybe even forgiven him, but he knew this missing child would reignite the hate for him. He picked up his pace and estimated that he could get home in about eighteen minutes.

Arthur Pennock wasn't his real name, he had been allowed to change his identity before moving to the area. The man formally known as Rodney Burroughs had spent twelve years in prison for child sex offences including kidnap. There was a TV on behind the counter in the shop and he had just seen the breaking news report scrolling across the bottom of the morning breakfast show. It told of a boy going missing.

He didn't see it coming; he didn't see the fist that broke his nose. He collapsed to the ground, and the next thing he felt was a kick to the stomach.

"Where is he? What have you done with him, you sick fucker?" demanded Simon Bray, the local man who fancied himself as being the top dog in the village.

"I haven't done anything, I…" Another kick silenced him.

Bray knelt down and put his hand around Arthur's throat. "Tell me or I'll fucking kill you."

Bray was so fixated on Arthur that he was not aware of the two police officers behind him. They pulled him off, dragged him away and read him his rights.

"You're fuckin' arresting me?" he screamed. "You should be arresting that sicko."

One of the officers helped Arthur to his feet. "Clear off back home, we'll talk to you later." The local police were aware that Arthur may become a target and had been keeping a discrete eye on him. They had done their duty in arresting the attacker, but even they couldn't hide the contempt they felt for the man.

An officer approached Griffin. "As we suspected might happen, sir, Arthur Pennock was assaulted this morning. The assailant is in custody."

Griffin was not at all surprised by this. "How bad was it?"

"Mr Pennock has a broken nose and bruising from a couple of kicks."

"Let me guess, it was Simon Bray."

"Yes, it was, sir."

"Where is Arthur now?"

"At home."

"Did he require hospital treatment?"

"He refused all treatment, sir."

Detective Griffin was well aware of Arthur's crimes but had spoken to the man and his social worker many times and believed him to be reformed. He had done his time, expressed his remorse and regret and paid his debt to society as the law required. But still, Arthur's crimes were monstrous and even Griffin couldn't help the feeling of disgust he felt for the man. Though his duty was to uphold the law, and a crime had been committed against Arthur. "I'll go and speak to him. Keep Simon Bray in a cell until I get back."

The detective heard the security bolt being drawn back, and a nervous-looking Arthur peered around the edge of the door. Griffin knew that the man had a wedge under the door to stop it from being kicked in.

"I know you didn't do it, Arthur, so let me in."

A couple more security chains were released and the door opened. Both of Arthur's eyes were black and his nose was obviously broken. He beckoned Griffin through to his living room, gesturing to a chair. Arthur sat opposite him with his head in his hands.

"We have your attacker in custody. Do you want to press charges?"

Arthur shrugged with an air of resignation. "What for?" he grunted, then snorted, trying to clear the blood from his nose. A bin full of bloodied tissues was testament to the damage that had been done.

"You were assaulted in an unprovoked attack."

"Some people assert that just me being here is a provocation."

"Even so, it is your right to press charges."

"And what purpose would it serve?" snapped Arthur angrily. "Other than to advertise that there's a sex offender living in the area?" He looked away, scowling, shaking his head. "A former sex offender," he grunted indignantly. He huffed and his shoulders dropped. "No one's going to believe me, are they?"

"Probably not. I've seen all the reports on you, and I've read the reasons why you were recommended for early release, but what you did stays with people."

Arthur hung his head. "I'm on the register for another five years, so I can't even defend myself." There was a long pause, then he looked up at the detective. "Have you found the boy?"

"No. Look, Arthur, it's important that you be completely honest with me; do you know anyone who might have kidnapped the boy?"

"NO!" shouted Arthur resentfully. "I don't know anyone, I don't talk to anyone. I know that people think there's a paedo network, but if there is, I'm NOT part of it!" He got up and grabbed his computer and mobile phone, shoving them at the detective. "Go on, take them, analyse them. Read all my emails, check my search history, look at all those hidden sectors that record everything. Check my call logs. I never delete anything, because I know that sooner or later it'll all be looked at, and you'll see that I have nothing to hide. It's just gardening, shopping and recipes. And no, I haven't got a burner phone hidden somewhere. If you don't believe me then send a search team in, turn the place upside down, rip up floorboards, that wouldn't be anything new for me. Dig the garden up if you feel you have to!"

It was obvious to Griffin that this burst of anger was Arthur's shame and the disgust he still felt for himself. The detective waved him down. "Sit down, Arthur, I don't need to see those."

He sat down, seething. "The news report said that the boy went missing at around ten last night. At about nine forty-five I spoke to my social worker for about fifteen minutes, she is pleased with my progress. Then I was on the phone to my former parole officer. He moved to Australia not long after I left prison, and I always speak to him on the anniversary of my release. He helped me come to terms with my crimes; he made me realise that I could change, he did more to help me than anyone has ever done. I was on the phone to him for well over an hour. I told the constables that last night."

"I know, and we have checked with both of them; they corroborate your story. You are not a suspect, Arthur, you have been ruled out."

Arthur sat shaking his head and snorting angrily, grabbing another tissue and wiping the last flecks of blood away. "It doesn't matter." He jabbed a finger in the direction of the village. "That lot, to them I'm their prime suspect." He looked at the detective, his anger dissipated and was replaced with resignation. "I'm going to have to move; no doubt I'll get a brick through my window tonight."

"I'll get a car to make a couple of passes tonight."

"Humpf!" grunted Arthur. "Your colleagues hate me too," he snarled, then he thought about the offer. "Sorry, I was being ungrateful. Thank you."

"Will you move?"

"Yes, I can't stay here anymore."

"Do yourself a favour, Arthur, don't leave right away. I understand your anxiety, but it will look like you're running away and that will fuel even more suspicion, and I will have a job keeping a lid on that. I will make sure that a car comes past at irregular intervals, that way no one will be able to establish a pattern."

"Thank you."

"One last thing, are you sure you don't want to press charges?"

Arthur sighed. "I don't want to press charges."

"Okay."

He left Arthur and made a call to the station instructing Simon Bray to be released without charge, and to be told that Arthur had been ruled out. He was also to be given a stern warning to stay away from Arthur and to not spread rumours. Simon refused to believe it and demanded that Arthur be arrested and charged but was ignored.

Griffin was on his way back to the wood when he received a call informing him that there had been a discovery.

Chapter 9
Remains

It was obviously that of a child and it could only be that of Darren Turner, but visual identification was impossible, it was just a skeleton. Flesh had been pared away from the bones, the skull had been smashed open and the brain was gone. All the internal organs were missing.

The searches had concentrated on routes out of the wood, roads, paths and bridleways had been followed. None of the searchers had gone into the heath, as there was no evidence of tracks through the gorse. It was only when the helicopter was making a wide turn taking it out over the stunted region that the discovery had been made.

A wave of depression washed over Griffin as he stood looking down at the bones.

"Who could do this?" he muttered to himself.

The lead forensic officer struggled to remain professional as he studied the remains and the area all around, confused by the scene. He looked up and saw the scavenging birds that would usually be the first to start pecking at what little remained of the flesh, but they weren't coming anywhere near and there was no evidence that they had before the boy was discovered. There was no insect activity and the flies that would normally be laying their eggs on a corpse within a couple of hours were noticeable by their absence.

It was too soon for putrefaction and the aroma of death that it causes, but there was so little flesh that he doubted whether this would happen. Also absent was any indication of a struggle, nor was there any evidence that anyone else had been there. An amount of blood that he considered to be consistent with that of a child, had soaked into the sandy soil, he pointed to it.

"With that amount of blood, the evisceration had to have happened here, and given the lack of any marks on the ground he was either unconscious or dead before it happened."

He looked all around at the dense gorse that surrounded the barren area, then back at the skeleton.

"There were no tracks in and no tracks out. No single animal could do this, it would have to be a pack, and their tracks would be obvious," he muttered. "The only disturbance is by us."

"Where are the internal organs?" whispered Griffin, the horror of the situation stealing his voice.

The forensic officer didn't hear the question, he was also horrified at the discovery.

"My first thought was of a big cat, an illegally held lion that has escaped and that the owners haven't reported. But, no, there'd be evidence and there just isn't any," he muttered, frustratedly as he tried to apply logic to make sense of the scene. He pointed to a blood-covered rock a little way off. "That must have been used to smash the skull open. The DNA on it will be the same as…" he pointed back to the skeleton. "…as that."

"Are you saying that a person did all this?"

"I don't know what I'm saying, but other than a human, the only animal that could wield a rock of that size would be a chimpanzee, and where is the evidence of one?" He gestured to the skeleton. "And that wouldn't explain this! A troop would have been needed."

The men studied the rock; with all that was wrong with this situation, the rock seemed particularly out of place.

"Why is there a rock here?" muttered Griffin. "The soil is sandy."

The two men forced the disgust from their minds and studied the bloodstained clothing.

"That's Darren Turner's football kit. It looks like some of it's been cut away with a knife while other parts have been ripped off." Griffin stood up straight, snapping back into detective mode. "Right, we need to get the surrounding area searched to see if we can find the missing body parts."

"I have an uncomfortable feeling that we're not going to find any."

"Are you saying that this boy was eaten?" Griffin didn't need a reply, it was obvious to him that this was the only explanation for the state of the body, but he had no explanation of how it could have happened.

Chapter 10
The Campaign

One Month Later

The initial shock at Darren Turner's death had faded to the point where people were getting on with their lives. There were still mutterings and theories on social media, but the police investigation had gone cold and other issues were now taking precedence.

One issue that had been slowly gaining ground was the idea of restoring the original name of the village back to Twinmere. Most people couldn't really see the point, but a few determined individuals had started a campaign; chief among them was Margo Middleton.

The instruments fell silent, and the last sentence of the last verse of the song was sung acapella:

"...and the mighty wave pulled the village down."

The well-connected force of nature that was Margo Middleton clapped enthusiastically as the song's final refrain faded away, and her clapping was an indication to the group to stop.

"Thank you, Shingle Beach, for the wonderful song, 'Twinmere Found' that has been written especially for the campaign by our two very own songstresses, Halo and Aura."

Margo had the natural ability to charm everyone she met, and her personality enabled her to easily take charge of any situation without coming across as bossy. She was blessed with a voice that commanded attention without being intimidating, and the sarcasm in her words to the band was subtle and only noticed by a couple of her close friends in the hall. They just managed to suppress their sniggering, as even the immaculate four part harmonies could not detract from the eight verses of cringingly awful lyrics and tortured rhymes.

Halo fiddled with her waist-length dreadlocks and shuffled on her feet, while her twin sister blushed. And while Halo embraced the hippy look, Aura tried, but was wearing designer jeans and had a Dolce and Gabbana clutch bag. The fourteen-year-olds were the daughters of the local folk group's lead singer, the bear-footed 'Mother Earth' styled character that called herself Spirit, and her guitarist husband, Eagle. Spirit beamed proudly at Halo and Aura, mouthing the words *'you're so talented'* at the blushing girls. Margo got up from behind the head table and made a point of moving to stand in front of the group, and this was her way of telling them, without actually telling them, that they were not to play anymore.

Foxmere village hall was packed for the first meeting of the Southmere renaming group. Seated at Margo's table was Joseph Sugden, a 'D' list actor from Ipswich who'd had walk-on parts in a couple of soap operas. He was adding his 'weight', as he liked to call it, to the campaign, but was secretly only there to bolster his chances of getting a role in an upcoming drama where one character was an environmental campaigner. It was a role that he desperately needed if he was to salvage his flagging career, and he was willing to do anything for it.

Margo was well aware of just how shallow he was, but he was young and quite good-looking, and would probably draw some young woman to the cause, so she would tolerate his barely suppressed ego—using him in exactly the same way that he was using her. Her plan was simple; she would suggest to someone that he becomes the face of the campaign, he would allow his name to be put forward but would then refuse to be the poster-boy, feigning embarrassment. He would appear to be reluctant to take on the role but would eventually allow himself to be talked into it.

There was an agitated muttering in the crowd, excited at the news of a special visitor who was going to lend his name to the campaign. People had seen the ivory white Bentley Continental in the car park and there was a lot of speculation as to who it might be. Margo straightened up, this action alone got people's attention and the light murmuring immediately died down.

"Ladies and gentlemen, no doubt you have all had your own ideas on the identity of our very special guest tonight. Well, let the conjecture cease as it is my honour to introduce to you Sir James Beaverton."

There was a collective gasp of surprise from the audience as she gestured dramatically to a curtain across a door which pulled back to allow Sir James to enter the hall. He made his way to Margo, respectfully accepting the applause that had erupted.

The well-loved, multi award-winning TV presenter had been a fixture on British television for just shy of sixty years, and although he presented a range of nature and natural world documentaries, it was well known that his passion was geology. Margo went and sat back down leaving Sir James standing by a seventy-five-inch television screen. He pressed a clicker in his hand and a presentation started. The first image was of the ruined homes on the beach at Wychborough.

Over the next two hours, and working without notes, he held the audience in thrall as he described the way erosion worked to shape the coastline. Sir James was one of those rare people that could take a dry-as-dust subject like geology and make it fascinating. His well-honed delivery making it seem that he was talking to each person individually instead of addressing an audience.

His two great skills were first, understanding that few people give much thought to geology, and that most people would comment on the colours of the layers in a cliff face, and all the while failing to appreciate the thousands of years of history that each band represented. The second skill was in making it interesting. All would leave the hall that evening with a different view of the world.

He spoke with a reserved passion, describing the action of the spring storm that had shifted so much sand to expose the village of Southmere, two miles out under the north sea. Murky underwater images of Southmere appeared on the screen, but what grabbed people's attention was the computer generated simulation taken from underwater scans. The village was so complete that an animation had been created, enabling the viewer to take a trip around the village, viewing it as it was hundreds of years ago before the disaster. People had been added into the streets and buildings and animated to give a human perspective to the story he was telling.

The last four pictures were a satellite image of the coast at Southmere; there was an audible gasp at one image which showed the estimated coastline at the time of the storm that took the village. The penultimate image was an image from an old map, clearly showing the name Twinmere, and the final picture was of that map overlaid on a top-down scan of the submerged village.

Sir James paused for effect, looked down for a few seconds, then back up at the audience, it was a practiced and effective move that added even more gravitas to his persona.

"All of this happened over five hundred years ago, so does it really matter? After all, it is all in the past, and so long ago. So should we bother to get the name changed back to what it was? How is it going to improve our lives?" he asked rhetorically, then again paused for effect. "But how far back do we have to go to correct an error? Two hours? yes, obviously. Two days? yes, of course. Two weeks? Yes, that would be reasonable, two years? That would also be reasonable. Two decades? Of course. So why not five centuries?" He left a pause for his words to sink in.

"Should we campaign for Southmere to return to its original name of Twinmere? Yes I think we should, because I believe in restorative history and that errors must always be corrected. Thank you."

This sentence was his cue to Margo that his presentation was done; she stood up and started the applause. Sir James nodded respectfully to accept the ovation then sat down.

Margo stood breathless for a moment, then composed herself. "Well, I think I speak for all here today, when I thank you, Sir James, for your wonderful presentation." Again, there was a light ripple of appreciative applause.

Margo turned to face the audience. "Who now thinks that we have no choice but to campaign to have the original name of Twinmere reinstated? Let's have a show of hands." No one kept their hands down.

"Okay, that's what I expected." She frowned slightly. "And now onto the vulgar subject of money." An amused groan rose from the audience. "All campaigns need a bit of money, not much though, as I fully intend to pull in as many favours as I can, and Sir James is going to use his influence to bring in some serious voices. But all donations will be gratefully received, and all proceeds for the sale of 'Twinmere Found' by Shingle Beach will go directly to the fund as will a percentage of the sale price of Sir James' book 'Written in Stone', his memoir of a life in the ground."

"A bank account has been set up, and I have to say right now, that the financial records will be open for anyone to examine. You will all receive a text with the bank details, should you wish to donate. If you do, then thank you in advance, but I understand that finances for some people are tight, so no one with think badly of you if you can't give anything. Should there be a surplus of funds after our mission is over, then all depositors will be asked to nominate a charity, and any excess cash will go to the one that receives the most votes."

"Thank you all for coming, updates will be posted on all the social media channels, so do check them regularly and have a safe journey home."

A general hubbub rose as people started to drift away. Margo smiled to herself as she watched as Aura made a B line for Joseph Sugden and stood looking up at him with big doe eyes, with Joseph basking in the adulation he was receiving, but trying hard to not look like he was basking in the adulation. While this was going on, Halo picked up a mandolin and tried to play an old Bob Dylan song. Spirit and Eagle opened a suitcase by the door and gestured to rows of CDs. There were two; one was a recording of the song played earlier, with the reiterated promise that all the money from that sale would go to the campaign. People were quite happy to pay the nine pounds for the terrible single, if only as a way of giving money to the cause.

The other CD was a collection of original songs written by Halo and Aura and performed by Shingle Beach. The overproud parents told everyone that they should buy it because Halo and Aura were soon going to be famous, hinting at a festival appearance, that was, in reality, just a gig at a village fete. There were a couple of polite purchases of the CDs with people handing over fifteen pounds for a recording of ten songs that they knew would all be appallingly bad and would be listened to once then never played again.

By contrast, everyone wanted to buy a signed copy of Sir James Beaverton's book on his life in geology.

The last of the attendees had gone, Shingle Beach had packed up and left, and the only people in the hall were Margo, Sir James and his chauffeur, who also doubled as his bodyguard. Father O'Sullivan had waited outside and watched them all leave, there couldn't be too many pairs of ears for what he had to say. A surprised Margo looked up at him as he entered.

"Father O'Sullivan, it's a bit late and I'm afraid you've missed the presentation. But I can come and see you tomorrow and fill you in on the details if you want—"

"You must not change the name," interrupted the priest.

"What? Whyever not?"

"You will put everyone in grave danger if you do." His voice was urgent and demanding, his expression equally so.

Sir James' chauffeur looked on suspiciously, he doubted whether there was a direct threat to Sir James from the frail old man, but he could not be sure and prepared himself in case he needed to act.

Margo looked at Sir James, then back at the priest and frowned deeply. "What danger?"

"I cannot tell you," he shouted. "The bishops were right to change the name, you must not change it back."

The chauffeur wasn't to going wait for an incident, he stood up and went to the priest, ushering him to the door. "I think you need to leave, sir."

"If you change the name, you will risk unleashing a horror that you simply can't imagine," called the Father as he was guided firmly out of the building. But he knew they would never believe him. Had this been thirty years ago when his deep resonant voice carried authority, then they may have done. His voice now was tremulous and had a higher pitch, it was that of an old man whose time was nearly up. He wanted desperately to tell them exactly what happened to the boy, but that would be too dangerous, there would be far too many questions, and some of his answers may be believed.

The chauffeur guided him out of the door and closed it. Margo looked apologetically at Sir James. "I am sorry about that, he is very old and sometimes old people get confused."

"You are being kind, Margo, what you are avoiding saying is that he has dementia." Sir James contemplated his own advancing years and the loss of his wife ten years previously. "Age is a cruel mistress, she takes the ones you love, then she takes your mind."

Outside, Father O'Sullivan sank to his knees clutching his cross. "Guide me, oh Lord, I know that I haven't got much time left, but I must protect these people, they do not understand the danger that they could release. O heavenly Father, I beg you to guide me, for I know not what to do."

Inside, Sir James turned to his chauffeur. "Find out how he got here and if necessary, drive him home. I will wait here with Margo, we have a few things to discuss."

"You walked three miles?" said the astonished driver.

"Yes, my effort is insignificant against the warning I had to bring."

"Whatever," grunted the driver. "Get in, I will drive you home."

"Thank you." The priest got in and realised that it was pointless talking to this man and sat silently praying for guidance. Orla was waiting for him, and the driver noticed that she had the same anxious expression. He thought no more of it, turned the car around and went back to the village hall.

The next morning, Father O'Sullivan had a slight spring in his step and felt cheerful.

"You're quite perky, Father. This is the first time I have seen you smile since… it happened."

"I had a wonderful dream last night, a voice kept telling me *you have done enough*."

"Well, Father, you have told the bishop and you have tried to warned people. There's not much more you can do."

"You're right, if I were younger and had more energy then maybe I could do more."

"That walk you did last night, it tired you out. But you wouldn't listen when I told you not to."

"Yes, it did make me tired, but it was something that I simply had to do. I feel invigorated now."

"Well, you go and sit in your favourite chair, and I'll bring you a nice cup of tea and a couple of biscuits."

He reached down and took hold of her hand. "You know, Orla, I have appreciated everything you have ever done for me over the past sixty years. But I don't think I have ever told you enough times how grateful I am for your kindness and the sacrifices that I know you have made for me."

Tears welled in the old woman's eyes as she watched him turn and leave the room.

Ten minutes later, Orla entered the sitting room to see the priest sitting, eyes open and smiling. "Here's your tea, Father, and I've got you some of your favourite biscuits. Now, your tea's hot so let it cool for a bit, you don't want to be burning your mouth now, do you?"

He didn't respond, he just sat staring straight ahead.

"Father, are you alright?"

Again, there was no response from him. Alarmed, she went to him and gently shook his shoulder. He didn't look at her, but slowly slumped forward, eventually falling out of the chair and onto the floor.

The paramedic finished his initial examination and turned to the weeping Orla. "He had a massive cardiac arrest, there was nothing you could have done."

"Did he feel any…?"

"He felt no pain, the expression on his face shows us that."

"I knew the Lord would call him as soon as he told me of his dream, but I never thought it would be today."

Chapter 11
The MP

"So, I can count on your support?"

For anyone else, this would be a question, but for Margo Middleton, it was an instruction to Giles Canham, the local member of parliament. She, like everyone else, knew that he was not a native of Suffolk and had been parachuted in at the last election to replace Angela Stradbroke, the disgraced former MP, who had quit before the investigation of cash for questions forced her out. As such, Giles was keen to be seen to be doing all he could for the county. Although he felt that the name change was not the most pressing issue for the region, though it would not involve too much effort on his part and might improve his chances at the next election.

"Of course, Margo. I will take it up with the Home Secretary personally."

"Thank you, Giles. Now, you have my number, so I look forward to you informing me of the outcome of your meeting with the her. I assume that it will be soon?" Again, this was more of a directive than a question. "Because we are less than a year away from a general election and the Home Secretary will soon be very busy trying to get legislation through, so a conversation with her in short order will help everyone."

The meeting with Giles had lasted an hour and he had felt browbeaten by Margo, though it had been subtle with demands phrased as polite requests and skilfully veiled references to his re-election chances.

"Rest assured, Margo, I will get my secretary to speak to the Home Office staff and find a diary date, though as you must appreciate, that may not be for a few…"

"Days?" she interrupted.

"I'm sorry, Margo, but it may not be for a few weeks, as I know the Home Sec is very busy right now."

She fixed a stare on him, making him feel uncomfortable.

"But I may be able to swing a brief chat with her."

"Thank you, Giles. Good day."

Margo left and he sat stunned; he wasn't used to being given the run-around and felt glad that she wasn't an opposition MP that he would have to face in the Commons.

Angela Stradbroke had been an anti-elitist, anti-patriarchy activist with slight anti-monarchy leanings and had enjoyed a high level of popularity with female voters. This was even after evidence of long-term bribery and corruption came to light that had exposed her receipt of large amounts of money from the very organisations she claimed to be against. Her supporters seemed to be overly forgiving of her, bordering on adulation to the point of dismissing the evidence as a fabrication by the newspaper that broke the story. Angela hadn't denied the allegations, hadn't threatened to sue the newspaper and had even alluded to the accusations as being true, but these facts were not discussed by her supporters.

Under Ms Stradbroke, the seat had enjoyed a healthy majority at the polls and had grown during her two terms. Giles realised that he would not get anywhere near the percentages that she had enjoyed from her near cult-like followers. Margo had indicated that a lot of the former MP's allies were also supportive of the name change campaign, so it would be in his interest to act swiftly. She subtly suggested that he would then be able to turn it to his advantage.

Chapter 12
The Crossword

Two Months After Darren's Body Had Been Found

"Only a few left," said Celia Jones as she sat doing the last crossword in the book. "Positively articulate, three letters starting with 'T'."

"Huh?" grunted her husband, Richard, not taking his eyes off the war documentary on TV.

"Positively articulate, three letters beginning with the letter 'T'."

"Oh, you do like your cryptic crosswords, don't you."

"Yeah, it keeps my brain active. Come on, help me out."

He smirked. "Hmm. So, what you're saying is that it doesn't keep your brain all that active," he teased.

She looked over the top of her glasses at him and huffed. "You know what it is, don't you!" she grumbled.

"Yep." He exaggerated a smug expression. "As a matter of fact, I do."

"In that case, don't tell me, I want to work it out for myself. And there's no need to look quite so pleased with yourself, mister smarty-pants."

She ignored his chuckling and focussed again on her book. "Fifteen down; slight sibling from Suffolk with an old name, eight letters," she muttered, puzzling over it for a few moments. Then quickly scanned over to the non-cryptic clues and immediately felt as though she was cheating.

"Former name of Southmere," she mumbled.

"Are you asking me?"

"No, I'm talking to myself."

"Okay. I had to ask because sometimes you mumble and you're talking to yourself, and sometimes you mumble and you're talking to me, and I never know which is which," he teased.

"Oh shush."

He watched her out of the corner of his eye, smirking as she struggled with the last four clues.

"Fifteen across, six countries could meet here, ten letters, all one word, so it can't be the United Nations, and anyway that's thirteen letters," she muttered.

"Are you talking to me this time?"

"No!"

Celia sat scratching her head for a few minutes, then looked at her husband again. "You know what this one is as well, don't you!" she grumbled with a slightly irritated tone to her voice, annoyed that she couldn't work it out.

He laughed. "Well, yeah, but what am I supposed to do? Pretend I don't know?"

She thought about it for a few moments, then gave up. "Okay, clever clogs, what is it?"

"Twickenham."

"Twickenham! How did you work that one out?"

"Another word for 'Countries' is 'Nations'. The Six Nations is a rugby tournament, and Twickenham is one of the venues where they would meet. At first I thought it could be Murrayfield, but that's eleven letters."

Celia filled it in then studied the remaining clues. "Okay, so fifteen down starts with a 'T'."

He smirked at her. "Are you going to look it up?"

"No, I'm not," she exclaimed, faking a bit of indignance, but realised that she probably would have to look it up. "I'm not going to look it up, I can't, because they don't print the answers to this crossword in this edition, they print them in the next one. Besides, I want to work it out from the other clues. Twenty-three across. A creature that blasts in from a compass point. It's got an 'A' in the middle, it's something, something 'A' something 'T'."

"Beast!" said Oliver, their nineteen-year-old son, as he walked past the door on his way upstairs.

"What?"

"Beast from the east! Come on, Mum, that was an easy one."

"Well, beast fits, and that would make fifteen down start with 'T' and end with 'E'."

"Any other clues?"

"Seventeen across, lightbulb moment, four letters."

"Idea?" he muttered.

"Okay, that was a bit too easy, so it may be wrong, but it fits. Nineteen across: Canadian animal that you eat with a spoon, five letters."

Again, she puzzled over the question, then glanced over at Richard who was smirking again. She frowned, a bit annoyed with herself that she was having to ask for his help.

She sighed. "Go on then, what is it?"

"It's Moose!"

"What! How on earth do you get that one?"

"Moose. It's a homophone."

"It's a what?"

Oliver poked his head around the door, chuckling. "It's what a gay bloke uses to look up partners on dating apps."

Richard frowned at his son. Oliver faked a hurt look. "What? I wasn't being disrespectful."

Richard ignored him and turned to his wife. "A homophone is a word that's spelled differently and has a different meaning to another word but pronounced the same way, like 'there' as in a different place, and 'their' as in belonging to someone. You'd eat mousse with a spoon, and a Canadian animal is a Moose."

"So that makes fifteen down, 'T' space, 'I' space, 'M' space, space, 'E'. So, what is a slight sibling from Suffolk? I reckon the clue is in the word 'slight', what's another word for 'slight' ending with an 'E'?" she asked herself. "I reckon that's 'mere'."

"Twinmere," said Christina, their fourteen-year-old daughter, as she finally looked up from her phone. "We did a bit in class on coastal erosion and learned about the village that used to be there, but it got washed away. Everybody used to think it was called Southmere, but a really old map of the area was found and it's old name was Twinmere. There's a campaign to have the old name reinstated."

Celia filled in the clue, then looked up and glowered at her husband. "Come on then, tell me what 'positively articulate' is."

"The."

"What?"

"*The!*"

"The what?"

"*The* is a definite article in a sentence."

"Okay, that makes the last three, 'The Twinmere Beast'; there, all done," said Celia as she closed her book. "Now, who wants a cup of tea?" She thought about the last three clues and chuckled. "Hmm, it sounds like a monster."

Everyone in the room shivered. "Ooh, can you feel that? It's suddenly got cold," grumbled Christina as she pulled on her hoody. "Can we have the fire on?"

Now that Father O'Sullivan was no longer around for her to look after, it had been decided that Orla was to move to a convent to see out her last days, and to be cared for by the nuns as she had cared for the Father. She was busy packing her things in a suitcase when she suddenly shuddered as a chill swept through her. "Oh no!" she gasped.

Vapour once again rose from the ground, gradually the face of the beast formed, it's eyes snapped open and turned southwest to Helmwood on the north-western outskirts of London where the Jones family lived.

"So soon," came its rumbling voice, "and so far." It started the long journey, drifting through the scrublands and out into the fields, its spectral body slowly taking on a corporeal form as it travelled through the night. As the sun rose, it became a vapour again and settled down into the ground, waiting for the sun to set so it could resume its journey.

It would take the beast four nights to cover the distance, but it had been called and had to find the caller. It travelled away from the lights of urban areas, sticking to fields, woods and hedgerows. It could tolerate moonlight; in centuries past, it could move freely at night, but there was much more light at night now; harsh, artificial light that burned its skin.

Four days later and the family was enjoying their usual evening routine. Celia put her iPad down and stood up. "Who wants a cup of tea?"

"Ooh, yes please dear," Richard answered, not looking away from the program he was watching.

"Oliver, do you want a cup of tea?" she shouted up the stairs.

"No thanks, Mum, I'm going out soon."

"Going out? It's nearly half past nine!"

Richard chuckled. "We were like that once, Celia, remember?"

She went into the kitchen and put the kettle on. "I'm just going to put the recycling out," she shouted through to the living room. A few seconds later, Richard's phone lit up letting him know that something had triggered the video doorbell; he checked the screen to see his wife placing the bags down and turning to come back in. He put the phone down and went back to the program he was watching.

A bare-chested Oliver ran down the stairs leaving the heady aroma of far too much aftershave trailing behind him. "Mum, do you know where my new shirt is?"

"She's making a cup of tea," replied Richard.

Christina looked up from her phone, stared at the door to the kitchen and frowned. "She's been doing that for a long time, Dad."

"She's probably tidying up the kitchen, you know how she likes it all spick and span in the mornings."

"Yeah, Dad, but for half an hour?"

Richard suddenly realised that there had been two commercial breaks in his program; he checked his watch, she had been gone for well over half an hour. Puzzled, he got up and went to the kitchen to find the back door open.

"Celia?"

No reply. He looked outside to see the recycling bags by the side of the road, but no sign of his wife. He went to the road and called out for her.

"Celia? CELIA!"

Christina appeared with a torch in her hand and the pair looked all around; after a few moments, Christina noticed something.

"Dad! There's blood!"

"Oh God! She must have been hit by a car." It was an illogical thing to say, as there was no evidence of a car coming across the wide greensward to the front of their property, but it was his first thought. He pointed down the road. "You look that way, I'll look this way." He suddenly realised that his daughter was far too young to be on her own at this time of night, and probably not emotionally strong enough to deal with a situation if she found her mother and that something unpleasant had happened. "No, don't, get your brother, you stay inside." He went to his frightened daughter and held her. "This is probably not her blood; we don't know where it's come from, it's most likely to be animal blood."

Richard and Oliver started to search, getting more and more frantic as time went on. Neighbours heard Richard calling her name and the son calling out for his mother. Soon, there were people from all along the road out searching. After an hour, Richard went inside and called the police, then remembered that Celia had triggered an alert from the video doorbell. He watched the playback and sat stunned at what he saw.

An Hour and Forty Minutes Earlier

The beast had reached the outskirts of Helmwood, making its way through the fields to avoid the streetlights. The yellow tinted white of these old lamps irritated its scales, but they were not as powerful as sunlight, so wouldn't burn. It got to the end of the road where Celia lived, turned the corner and was dazzled by the intense white light of the new LED streetlamps. With its eyes burning and skin scorched, it recoiled back into the shadows, but it could sense Celia's presence. It would need to be fast, but it knew that this would take a lot of its energy.

The beast made its move, scrambling over a car and hitting her side on with enough force to stun her, she was still conscious but dazed and unable to comprehend what had happened. It brought its claw up and slit her throat as it carried away her limp body, dashing through the street as the light burned its skin, and with blood pumping from her slashed artery.

<<<◇>>>

Police cars were outside with the blue lights flashing, officers had set up a perimeter and a few of the neighbours were standing back watching the events unfold; some just curious, some, mainly the women, were anxious. Others wondered if they were unwittingly in possession of that tiny, seemingly irrelevant piece of information that would help find her.

The blood on the ground had been sampled and a swab taken of the daughter's mouth to check for familial DNA to either confirm or dismiss the blood as being Celia's. Uniformed officers were taking statements from Oliver and Christina. Detective Inspector Alan Buckley was talking to Richard, probing with harder questions, the difficult questions that had to be asked.

"She's about five-five, and weighs about sixty kilos, erm, shoulder-length brunette hair," stammered Richard. He knew these were questions that needed to be asked but answering them was harder than he expected.

"What is your wife wearing, sir?" asked Buckley.

He hesitated for a moment, trying to recall today's clothes while making sure that he wasn't describing anything generic that she had on. "Erm, err, a blouse, a white blouse with a small floral print, it's, erm, quite distinctive. She's wearing ladies grey Levi's 501's and Nike trainers."

"Do you know if anyone would want to harm your wife?"

"No, nobody, everyone loves her."

The detective, having worked on a similar case a few years before, prepared himself for the next question. In the previous case, a fifty-year-old woman, a wife of thirty years and mother of three, had calmly walked out of the family home and got in the car of her secret lover. She had been found six weeks later on the other side of the country, alive and well and living with him.

"How are things at home, sir?"

"What do you mean?"

"Was your wife agitated or did she seem depressed? Did she have a problem with alcohol? I'm sorry to ask these questions, but we have to know all the facts."

"That's okay, I, erm, I understand. And no, she was completely normal. She drank very little, in fact, we don't even keep alcohol in the house."

"Has she seemed at all distant recently?"

Richard knew where this was heading. "Everything between us was fine, Officer. Celia was happy; we're a close family. Both Celia and I are fully engaged with the kids' futures. There's no way she would have walked out." He paused, wondering if he should say what he needed to say, or if he had got his wife totally wrong all these years. "There's no way she's gone off with someone else, no way."

Buckley made a note, but in the back of his mind, he recalled that those were almost the exact same words that the other husband had used.

Then Richard suddenly remembered the doorbell. "I can actually prove that she didn't get in a car!" He took his phone and opened the doorbell app. The video opened with the last file that Richard had viewed.

Buckley looked at the video playback. Celia was clearly visible dumping the bags, illuminated as she stood in the pool of light. She turned to walk back to the house, took a couple of paces then simply disappeared.

Seeing it again stressed Richard out and he sat down with his head in his hands. "I can't explain it, there must have been a glitch in the recording, some sort of gap and maybe she did get in a…" His voice trailed away as he tried not to think that she had walked out on the family.

The detective took Richard's phone and played the video again, this time watching the time display in the top right corner. He noticed that the time didn't glitch. "She was literally there one second and gone the next," he muttered to himself. He checked the make of the video doorbell and a quick search on the internet showed the record resolution to be 1080p at a rate of twenty frames a second, so the image quality was there, and when he compared the image against the front hedge, the width of the recorded scene was over fifteen metres. She was central in the frame, and he could think of no way an adult woman could cover the seven odd metres in less than a second from a standing start.

He was broken out of his concentration by a constable. He beckoned the detective outside. "We found some more blood, sir."

"Where?"

"Twenty-five metres away, sir." The constable paused, a concerned look on his face. "And again another twenty-five metres on."

Buckley left them to carry on with the search while other officers took statements. He needed to stay, but he felt that what was on the video was too important and here he didn't have the equipment to examine the video in enough detail, he had to get to the lab. Richard provided him with the login password so he could download the files from the night.

<<<◇>>>

Back at the station, he loaded the video files from the doorbell into the technical lab computer and pressed 'Play'. He watched intently, studying file after file for anything that might give him a clue as to what had happened. Cars passed, people passed, but none returned, no one was lingering or staring at the house, no cars cruised slowly back and forth with the occupants staring at the house.

Eventually, he got to the file where he saw Celia Jones walking with the recycling bags in her hand. She placed them down turned and started to walk back, and in an instant she was gone. She had not given any indication that she was concerned about anything, no nervous glances, no agitated body language; she walked calmly to the end of the drive, placed the bags down, then took two paces back and simply vanished.

He stepped the video back one frame at a time until he got to the point where she disappeared, then rewound a further four seconds, paused the video and hit the spacebar, each tap would advance the video by one frame. At the recorded frame rate of twenty per second, eighty taps would take him the four seconds to the point where she disappeared. Nothing happened until he had tapped the spacebar seventy-five times.

Suddenly, he saw a blurred image, he couldn't tell the colour, as the camera had switched to night vision, monochrome mode, but he could just about make out a shape, it looked a bit like a man galloping on all fours. He tapped the spacebar another three times and each time saw the blurred image. The last tap showed that whatever it was, it was now upright, and causing Celia's body jerk to sideways. The next four taps had her being carried away by something, her body also blurred, but obviously limp. The tap after that had her out of shot, gone in a twentieth of a second.

Puzzled, he did a quick calculation; ten frames represented half a second, and whatever it was that appeared then carried her away, covered fifteen metres in half a second, and seven of those metres seemed to be done carrying a sixty kilo woman. "That's over one hundred kilometres an hour," he said to himself. Unable to believe it, he did the calculation again and got the same result.

Putting this to the back of his mind, he stepped back to the point where the image first appeared. The angle of the shot showed that it was not a vehicle, it was definitely a body of some sort on the path. Though as he stepped through the next few frames, he was astonished at the speed it appeared to be travelling. The image of Celia just after she was taken was slightly different, it seemed like an arm had been raised and there was something lighter in colour on the end of it and vaguely curved; it was level with her neck.

The night vision mode had reduced everything to shades of grey, but though the subsequent three images of her were blurred by speed, there was an obvious black area around her neck that wasn't there before. Previous experience with night vision systems told him that this was blood, a lot of blood.

The report of the blood twenty-five metres away came to him again and he realised that this was the distance travelled between beats of her heart that would have pumped the blood out, so she was still alive at that point.

The beast had eventually found its way out of the bright lights of the town and was in a dark corner of a wheat field where it was consuming her. It couldn't wait, it needed the nutrition to give it the strength to heal the burns on its body where the scales had hardened and dropped off.

The sky was lightening by the time it finished and it was only a matter of minutes before the sun broke over the horizon. Satiated, its body dissolved and it drifted down into the ground.

The road was taped off and a line of police officers were on their hands and knees making their way along the road carrying out a fingertip search for anything out of the ordinary. They had gone a short way from where she disappeared when one of the officers put his hand up, then pointed to a piece of vaguely triangular material.

The detective placed it in an evidence bag then studied it. "Tortoiseshell?" he muttered to himself as he looked at the colours of the triangle that reminded him of a large guitar plectrum. He handed it to a forensic technician.

"Get that checked for DNA."

"Got another one," came the call from the officer. Something piqued the detective's interest. He took it and placed in in an evidence bag, holding it up. "Okay people, look for these. If my hunch is correct, it will lead us to Celia Jones."

He was correct, and five hours later, a skeleton was found in the corner of a wheatfield, and from its size, it was probably that of a woman. All the internal organs were gone and the flesh carved from the bones. The lead forensic officer pointed to the ripped clothes that were strewn about. "Some of these seem to have been cut off the body with a sharp knife, others torn away in what appeared to be a frenzied attack." He seemed as confused as the detective. "There's a fair bit of blood on the ground but nowhere near enough for a whole adult body."

"She must have bled out most of it."

Buckley looked at the clothes strewn all around. He checked his notes, but he didn't really need to, he knew that these were the clothes that Celia had been wearing.

"So, are we calling this?" muttered the forensic officer.

"Yeah, I'm prepared to say that this is Celia Jones, but get DNA testing done."

The two men stared down at the remains, both thinking the same thing. Both wondering how all of the body was gone except the bones, and more importantly, where the flesh had gone.

"There are no footprints."

"I'll inform Mr Jones." The detective got in his car and sighed as he drove the four kilometres back to the home.

As he got out of the car, the detective noticed that a little way down from the Jones's home, the son of one of the neighbours was studying some scratches and grumbling about dents on the bonnet of his car. It may be nothing, but it was so close to the location where Celia disappeared that it could be important. He made a mental note to speak to the lad later.

<<<◇>>>

A bleary-eyed Richard opened the door to a police detective who was trying to stay professional through obvious shock.

"Where are your children?"

"They're upstairs in their rooms trying to get some sleep." Richard could tell from the expression on Griffin's face that this was bad news. "You've found her, haven't you?"

"I need to speak to you alone."

Oliver appeared at the top of the stairs, rubbing the sleep from his eyes. "What is it, Dad? Have they found Mum?"

"I have to speak to the detective, you stay here and look after Christina, she needs you."

"But Dad…"

"Please Oliver, just stay here."

Richard closed the door and walked with Buckley, his shoulders hunched. Oliver was now at an upstairs window and saw the detective say something and watched in horror as his father's legs buckled. He wouldn't need to be told that his mother wouldn't be coming home, it was obvious. Richard left the detective and walked back to the house, his head in his hands. Oliver went to his sister's room, shaking her gently on the shoulder to rouse her.

"Come on, Chris, get up, Dad's got some news for us."

Richard stood facing his children, his shocked face slowly morphing into anguish. Oliver stood with his arm around his sister, and the pride Richard felt for the way his son was comforting her did nothing to erase the devastation he felt. There was silence for a few moments; eventually he spoke.

"Mum's not…"

"I know, Dad, I know."

Buckley didn't see the father break down, but he heard the howling. Shaking his head, he left them and went to the damaged vehicle. The young man was clearly annoyed at the damage to his car but was also aware of the bigger issue, as everyone had heard Richard's cries. The lad seemed embarrassed as he looked at his car. Buckley looked at the dents and scratches.

"When did this happen?"

"They weren't there when I got home at around nine-thirty last night, so between then and now." The young man shrugged. "It's nothing," he muttered. "I'll get it sorted, the dents will pull out, the scratches can't be polished away though, I'll have to get it resprayed."

Buckley paced around the vehicle, noting that the marks and scuffs went from the boot, over the roof, and onto the bonnet. Looking along the damage, he saw that it lined up exactly to where Celia had been.

"Do you have a video doorbell or CCTV."

"We've got a video doorbell."

"Does it record sound?"

"Yeah." The young man stood back, puzzled. "It's only a car, this is hardly important, what with Mrs Jones going missing."

"Even so, I'd like to see the files."

Buckley sat at his desk, stepping through the video files until he got to the one where he saw the lad's car arrive. The time stamp recorded this as just gone half past nine. The car was visible to the left of the screen, illuminated by the bright light from a streetlamp almost directly overhead. There was the general burbling of traffic in the distance, but this was a quiet part of town, low crime and peaceful, and a place where cars could be left on the street without fear of vandalism. It was just this fact that had drawn Buckley to the car in the first place.

He continued to watch, studying the car. Then it happened; at five to ten there was a sound, a thud. Below the video was the audio waveform that showed a spike. But the thud sounded wrong, it wasn't like one hit, more like several occurring at almost exactly the same time. He clicked on the audio wave and dragged the cursor to expand the timeline and quickly saw that there were three double thuds in less than a tenth of a second. Setting the cursor over the middle spike and looking at the video frame, he saw a blurred image, but it appeared to be exactly the same as the one in Celia's video.

He knew that this family's video doorbell and Celia's house doorbell were the same make and model and that their internal clocks took their time from the internet, so it was safe to assume that they were exactly the same. He had estimated the distance from the car to where Celia was last seen to be about twenty metres. If this thing going over the car was the same thing that hit her, and assuming that the time stamps were accurate, then the time difference between the car being hit and Celia being taken showed that whatever it was, it was travelling at over one hundred kilometres an hour.

Chapter 13
Skeleton

The officer from the social media monitoring unit handed a mobile phone to Buckley. "Sir, you need to see this."

The detective took the phone and saw the article that had been taken from a website and shared on social media. The number nine was at the bottom, meaning that it had already been sent to nine other people.

MISSING WOMAN'S SKELETON FOUND, was the headline banner of the 'news' section of a conspiracy theory website, one well known for its sensationalist stories and plain lies.

A subheading read: *The police are refusing to say whether or not this is the action of a cannibal cult!*

This website discovered that mother of two, Celia Jones, went missing last night and was found this morning. Her clothes had been ripped off and all the flesh stripped from her body, leaving just the skeleton that you see in the picture below. There is speculation that she may have been alive as it happened. Who knows what agony she suffered!

Why was she taken? What did she know about the rich and powerful men and women who do these things with impunity, the sinister cabals that this website knows to exist and are trying to expose. Celia Jones was just another one of their victims and...

The detective didn't read any more. It would be the usual conspiracy theory rubbish, but what he did notice at the bottom of the page was the inevitable *subscribe for more information, just a mere five pounds a month gets you the news that the paedophile-owned mainstream media won't publish.*

Below the text was the blurred image of what the detective knew to be a human skeleton. A tag on the image said, "click to reveal." He clicked it and saw the picture of the denuded skeleton taken from the air.

He sighed, realising that someone on the force had leaked information, then he remembered the helicopter. "They would have been tracking us as we moved along the road following the trail of blood and whatever those triangles were. They must have got the picture before we covered her up."

He immediately called Richard. "Where are your children?"

"They're upstairs in their rooms."

"Have you told them anything about the way Celia was found?"

"I didn't have to tell them, they knew she was dead. All I said was that her body had been found."

"Don't let them look at any social media."

"Why?"

"An image has been published and..." He stopped short as he heard Christina's anguished wail, clearly audible from the other end of the house.

"She's seen it, I'd better go to her," sighed Richard as he ended the call.

"Bastards," muttered the detective as he thought of the distress this would cause.

The social media monitoring officer took the phone. "What is wrong with these people?"

"There's always someone making money out of other people's misery," grunted Buckley. "We'd better hope that it doesn't go viral."

"Sorry, but it's already started. In the past few minutes, it's appeared on a couple of European sites and at least one US cable news organisation is running the story. It's only a matter of time before it's picked up by the mainstream over there, and they'll jump at the chance of a sick story from outside America."

The detective picked up his car keys. "I need to go and see the family."

Christina's eyes were bloodshot, standing out in stark contrast to her ashen face. She sat hunched in a chair, Oliver stood behind her, scowling as he rubbed her shoulders to comfort her. His anger seemed to be directed equally at his father and the detective.

"You said Mum's body had been found." His tone of voice was accusative with barely concealed anger. He held up his phone, showing the image from the website. "Is this how she was found?"

Buckley sighed. "I'm sorry, but yes." The detective braced himself for a reaction.

Christina burst into tears again, but Oliver stayed calm and looked at his father. "I understand why you couldn't have told Chris, but you could have told me, and I would have broken the news to her. Instead, she had to find out from social media."

Tears ran down Richard's face. "I'm sorry, Oliver, I did what I thought was best to protect both of you."

Christina wiped her eyes, swallowed hard and composed herself. She sat up straight and mustered as much dignity as her grief allowed. "We want to know what happened to Mum."

A wave of anguish came over their father as he realised he would have to relay to them things that he wanted to forget. "Please Chris, no."

"Chris and I have a right to know, Dad," snapped Oliver, firmly. "It's going to be all over social media tomorrow, people will speculate, and all the creeps will come out from under their rocks. God knows what's going to be said, so we need to know the truth, it's the only way Chris and I will be able to cope."

"I can't, I'm sorry." Richard looked over at the detective. "Can you tell them?"

Oliver looked at the detective. "It said that the police won't say if it..." he stopped and bent down to his sister. "Sorry Chris, but I have to ask."

She wiped away a tear, then looked up at her brother, seeming to take strength from him rather than her father who was starting to shrink down, his shoulders ever more hunched and his head bowed.

"That's okay, Oliver, we have to know, so ask him."

The young man straightened up, his face displaying a maturity beyond his years. "Was it cannibals?"

"No, absolutely not. The website that first published the story is just making things up. We haven't released any details to the media and what was posted is pure fantasy—sensationalism at your expense and with no regard to your feelings. We have been monitoring that website for some time, but I'm afraid we have no power to stop them. They stay just this side of the law and there's nothing we can do. And I'm sorry, but you are right, there will be horrible things posted and the next few days will be very difficult for you. I wish that there was a way I could protect you from it all, but I can't and all I can say is this: don't believe anything you read, and don't respond to the trolls."

"The picture was taken from a helicopter, we had just made the discovery and were in the process of covering it up, and I am truly sorry that we couldn't have done it quicker."

"But how can you be so sure it wasn't cannibals?"

The detective paused and thought about his words. "I don't want to say too much, but if a group of people were involved then there would be certain evidence at the scene, and that evidence just isn't there."

"How... how did she end up there, like that?"

"We just don't know, but I promise you that I will find out if it's the last thing I do."

"She was eaten though, wasn't she?" whispered Christina as she stared blankly at the wall beyond the detective. "I mean, there's just her bones. Where's the rest of her?"

"We don't know yet."

"Tell us everything." Oliver's voice was firm and demanding.

Christina reached up and took hold of Oliver's hand, then looked at the detective, her sorrow fading slightly, her brother's maturity feeding into her. She sat up straight, shook away her sorrow and looked directly at Buckley. "Yes, tell us what you think happened."

The detective looked over at Richard, who closed his eyes and nodded. "Tell them," he whispered through his grief.

"Your mother had put the recycling bags down and had taken two steps back when something grabbed her. We don't know what it was, but it was fast, and she disappeared from view in under a second."

Oliver scowled, confused. "But what could have done that? Someone on a motorbike?"

"That's possible, but I think it's highly unlikely. Any bike going that fast would have made a noise and there is nothing on the recording except vehicles in the distance. Plus, it would be near impossible to travel at that speed and sweep someone off their feet without crashing."

"In the field, was she dead when it happened?" demanded Christina.

Buckley thought of the amount of blood on the road and realised that losing so much would have been fatal. "I am certain that she was. I believe the impact of whatever it was would have knocked her unconscious." He paused, hoping this was true, then his phone beeped, breaking the flow. He took the phone and saw a message from the DNA lab confirming the blood to be a ninety-nine percent familial match to the sample provided by Christina. The blood was from Celia.

His shoulders dropped and he put the phone away. "That was the lab, the blood was your mother's. I'm sorry."

Christina's boldness faded and she whimpered; Oliver comforted her.

Buckley waited a few moments for her to calm down. "As for what else happened, well, we just don't know."

Oliver stared hard at the detective, a look that burned into him. "Well, you'd better find out then, hadn't you!"

The detective left them, he knew that the full impact was yet to hit all of them, the father was already starting to break down, the daughter would be next; there was only so much comfort her brother could give her. Oliver seemed to have grown as a man, he could be the rock that the other two would come to rely on. Though it was clear that he would eventually need support. He also knew that when the collapse comes, it will be dramatic for all of them.

As he got in his car, he remembered a story from a couple of months back where a boy's skeleton had been found. Back at the station, he did a bit of research then made a call.

Chapter 14
Similarities

"This is DI Alan Buckley, Helmwood CID. Is that DS Nigel Griffin?"

"Speaking, what can I do for you?"

"You are the investigating officer on the Darren Jones case, am I correct?"

Buckley heard a faint grunt of frustration, and there was a pause before Griffin spoke, "Yes I am." He sighed heavily, he knew that Buckley, like every other officer in the police and a lot of the general public, was aware that he had got nowhere. After all, it had been the top story on the national and international news for a week with him making uncomfortable appearances on TV appealing for information. Social media had lit up with the usual unhelpful mix of concerned people with irrelevant 'evidence', and the ignorant with their uninformed speculation. There were cries of police incompetence; armchair detectives spouted absurd conspiracy theories and other people posted the usual mix of unkind comments and hate. Due to the sheer horror and the lack of a suspect, it became a story that although fading, was still active, with posts every day.

Someone had lifted a picture of the family from Laura's social media account, and it had been shared widely. It was taken at a party and was one of those jokey pictures with Laura appearing to stumble while trying not to spill her glass of red wine. The parents were accused of being alcoholics who neglected their son; the implication, hinted at by some, stated openly by others, was that they were directly responsible for his death. Because of the picture, Laura received some particularly nasty online abuse, and from the tone of the posts, they had to have been posted by females.

Griffin, though in the midst of a very difficult investigation, had to make an appearance on national TV defending the family. Though the upshot of that was to just fuel claims of a coverup. It did nothing to stop the hateful comments and by drawing attention to them, actually made them worse. This was something that Buckley was aware of; he hadn't seen any of the posts but experience told him what they would have been like. He knew that there would be hate and ignorance surrounding Celia's case, though he was always appalled at the level of viciousness that women were capable of in their posts. He hoped Celia's family would heed his advice and avoid stories on social media.

"I hope you've got some information for me, because I've got jack shit!" grunted Griffin.

"Sorry, no, well, yes, possibly. Obviously, I know about your case, and I've got a case that has striking similarities. I'd like to meet up with you to discuss it because what I've got is a bit odd. Maybe we can help each other."

"I hope so, as right now, I'd do absolutely anything to get Darren Jones' case moving."

"I'll be with you first thing tomorrow morning."

The next morning, Buckley was at the Suffolk police station. Griffin frowned, his frustration obvious. "The closest I have to a witness is Darren's friend, Julius. He was with the boy in the tent, he came in frightened, claiming that Darren had told him a scary story. The mother sent him back out but when he got to the tent, Darren Jones was gone."

"Did he say what the story was about?"

"No, only that Darren had said something that he shouldn't have done."

"What was it?"

"Julius wouldn't say exactly, all he would say is that it was dangerous." Griffin sighed heavily. "There would be huge amounts of speculation on what happened to the boy, so Julius's parents decided that they had to tell him that Darren was dead. As soon as they told him that, he totally clammed up, he literally hasn't said a word since then. Total brain lock: he can't go to school, he doesn't watch TV, doesn't listen to anything or read anything, he just sits in silence staring into space. He hardly eats. Specialist child protection officers have tried to get him to talk. Child psychologists have tried, doctors, nurses, us, his parents, everybody has tried, but nothing works. The psychologist suspects that if he doesn't start talking soon, well, it could be permanent."

"The parents are beside themselves with worry." Griffin's shoulders dropped. "Julius's father got himself arrested a couple of days ago. He got in a fight. Someone said to him that the Turners were bad parents, and that was a trigger that didn't need to be pulled. The guy he attacked wants to press charges." He shrugged. "It's his prerogative, but all it will do is light up social media and get the press camping outside the Turners' house again."

"You said yesterday that you've got jack shit in the way of evidence; so, what *have* you got?"

Griffin opened the case file and was unable to hide his exasperation. "The gist of it is general statements from the adults. There's the limited statement from Julius, Darren's friend who had been with him but left to go inside because he got frightened. The mother said Julius had said something about a monster but she couldn't add anything else meaningful. The mother sent him back out, but when he got to the tent, the Darren Turner was missing. There's a couple of seconds of CCTV, and these things."

The image of the triangular objects appeared. "DNA testing on these came back as 'undetermined'. It's animal but doesn't match anything. So there must have been an error in the testing. They've been sent to another lab to see if they can determine what sort of animal it is."

"We have things that look exactly the same."

Griffin's head snapped up. "Are you getting them tested for DNA?"

"Yeah, and from the looks of them, I'm willing to bet that they're a match to the ones you have."

"Oh my God!"

"Can I see the CCTV recording?"

"Sure."

Buckley studied a slow-motion playback of the two second clip of the thing in the light beside the tent, confused as to what he was looking at, Griffin noticed.

"Yeah, we don't know what it is either, and the adults walked all over the area while they were looking for the boy, so no footprints."

"I don't think you'll find any anyway," muttered Buckley.

"What do you mean by that?"

"I'll tell you later." He pointed to the section of video where there seemed to be steam or smoke coming from whatever it was that they were looking at. "It looks like a couple of things have dropped off."

"Yeah." Griffin pulled up the image of the two triangles again. "I think they're these." He looked curiously at Buckley. "What are the similarities between this case and yours?"

"A woman went missing two nights ago; her skeleton was found yesterday morning stripped of all flesh and internal organs. There's no sign of a struggle, so we're pretty sure she was dead, but there's no sign of anything else either. No footprints, nothing. She was found in the corner of an unharvested wheat field with no tracks in or out."

Griffin sighed. "Darren Turner was found in a clearing in an area of dense gorse and fern bushes, no tracks in or out of that either. The clearing was weird, all the foliage was stunted and deformed, and no animals would go in it, birds wouldn't fly over it."

"The wheat was flattened around Celia Jones' body, but for a couple of metres beyond that the wheat left standing was withered and looked diseased." Buckley thought for a bit. "You said there was a limited statement from Julius; what did he say?"

"What he didn't say is more important. All he said was that Darren had said something that he shouldn't have done and that it was dangerous, and there was his 'monster' comment. We really want to know what that was, but like I said, he won't speak at all now, he hasn't uttered a word since being told that Darren was dead. Three child psychologists have assessed him, and all say that he is unlikely to ever speak again."

"What could have been said that was so bad?"

"Whatever it was, there's no doubt in my mind that it led directly to Darren Turner's death." Griffin huffed, irritated by the illogical situation. "Even if he named a child-killer, that still wouldn't account for where the body was found and the state it was in."

Griffin shuffled awkwardly in his chair, seeming to struggle with something. "The thing is Darren's parents told me that he had a vivid imagination and was known to come up with fantastical stories. They also said he liked to say things to scare Julius. So, I've had to factor that in as well."

Chapter 15
An Uncomfortable Thought

Buckley sat at his desk in the Helmwood station thinking through everything. Ever since talking to Griffin, he'd had a strange feeling about the case. There just were too many similarities. His mind kept drifting back to the dents on the car. He'd studied them at the time but had tried to not make that obvious. He hadn't taken a picture, as he didn't want to draw attention to them because they could be completely irrelevant and a distraction from the search for Celia Jones.

While the lad wasn't looking, he had placed his hand over a few of the dents. Each one was bigger than his palm, and each one had four scratches in line with where the tips of his fingers would be, but about eighty to one hundred millimetres further on. He thought back to the image that appeared to be a claw reaching up to her neck followed by the black area in the next image.

Again, the speed came to him; he knew that a cheetah can reach those speeds, but only in short bursts and would certainly not be able to carry a sixty-kilo woman. Also the dents and scratches in the car were also not consistent with a cheetah's paws.

An email notification broke him out of his thoughts. It was from the lab, confirming the DNA from the objects to be the same as the ones that Griffin had, that they were animal in origin, but that the DNA profile didn't match any species in the database.

Over the course of the next few days, it became obvious to him that the case was going to go cold. There were no witnesses and what few clues he had made no sense. Like Griffin's investigation of Darren Turner's death, there were so few leads that the investigation was going to be scaled back as new crimes emerged that needed to be investigated.

But Buckley found himself dwelling on the DNA report, his thoughts bordering on obsession. He tried to get the video files enhanced, though the results were no better than the original and proved inconclusive. But something was definitely there, something that moved faster and for longer than any other animal.

"Could this be an undiscovered species?" he muttered to himself. "Sensible, well-adjusted people insist they have seen big cats in the countryside, but no evidence is ever found for them. Is it possible that in the twenty first century there are still land animals to be discovered in Britain?" The more he tried to tell himself no, the more doubt entered his mind.

"Only about twenty-five percent of the oceans have been surveyed, and there must be monsters in the deep that have yet to be found." He suddenly remembered what Julius had said. "The boy said that Darren had said something dangerous and that it was about a monster."

Unable to believe his illogical train of thought, he picked up the phone to call the Jones' home.

"What!" snapped Oliver as he snatched up his father's phone and saw the detective's name.

"This is Detective Buckley. Can I speak to your father?"

"You could try, but he's asleep. He drank a whole bottle of whiskey this morning."

Buckley could hear the irritation and disappointment in the son's voice, tinged with a hint of disgust.

"We need Dad to be on it, I'm okay at the moment," growled Oliver. "But Christina's a mess and Dad getting drunk is not helping."

"It's going to be hard for all of you, hopefully this will be a one-off, but if it happens again, let me know and I'll see if I can get some help for you."

"Thanks. Anyway, what did you want to talk to him about?"

"Do you know what your mother had been doing immediately prior to the event? I'm sorry, Oliver, I can't really put it any other way."

"Yeah, I get that. She went to the kitchen to make a cup of tea and put the recycling out…" Oliver's voice faded as he thought of his mother's last moments.

"What was the evening routine like in your home?"

"It was pretty much the same every night. Dad would watch documentaries on TV, I'd be upstairs getting ready to go out, Chris would be on her phone or her iPad and Mum would be doing a crossword." There was a pause and a deep sigh from the young man. "She always liked to do those really big ones." There was another pause. "But thinking about it, she'd finished the crossword and hadn't done one for a few days."

Buckley thought hard about his next question. "Do you know if she said anything unusual in the days leading up to…"

Oliver sighed wearily. "It's alright, you can say it."

"This is going to sound odd, but in the days before her death, did she say anything about a monster?"

"A what!"

"I know it's a strange question, but did she?"

"I don't know, I was always upstairs getting ready to go out. Dad and Chris were usually in the room with her."

"I don't suppose you still have the crossword?"

"Yeah, probably, we've not exactly been in the mood for tidying up."

"I'll call by and pick it up, if I may."

"Yeah, whatever."

Buckley had hoped that the crossword was in a paper, but it was in a puzzle book, all had been filled in and he had no way of knowing which one Celia had been working on. Oliver didn't know, and getting any sense out of Richard and Christina was out of the question. Richard was rambling as a result of drink, she was rambling as a result of grief, with neither of them adding anything coherent.

Chapter 16
The Letter

"The Italian ambassador is here to see you, Home Secretary." Camilla Moreno, the UK Home Secretary, was a third-generation economic migrant whose ancestors came over from Spain to escape the repression of General Franco's rule. She had risen to almost the very top of her party, being just one small step away from becoming prime minister. She was hailed as the product of hard work and determination that a motivated migrant can bring to the country. She was held up as a shining example of positive immigration that had a direct benefit for Britain. Though she was now tasked with stopping immigration. A task that she clearly seemed to relish.

She looked up at her private secretary. "Why? Our meeting on the migrant crisis is scheduled for tomorrow afternoon."

"Ambassador Moretti says that this is not about tomorrow's meeting, it is another matter, and is of great urgency and importance—his words, Home Secretary."

Camilla frowned, an unscheduled visit like this was unlike the supremely organised Moretti. "Well, you'd better show him in then." She closed her dispatch box and waited for her guest.

An elegant man entered; blue-eyed, with dark hair shot through with grey. He was immaculately dressed in five thousand pounds worth of a slate-grey Brunello Cucinelli two piece suit; no doubt his silk shirt would be pushing four hundred, and the silk tie that perfectly contrasted with the grey of the suit would be nudging two hundred. The next thing she noticed were his shoes: a pair of black Ferragamo penny loafers, a snip at over a thousand pounds a pair. Then she thought about her salary and the kind of clothes she bought, expensive for her, but humble by comparison to his.

She stood to meet him, holding out her hand and shaking his warmly. "Giacomo, what a pleasant surprise."

"It is a pleasure to see you too, Camilla, though the reason for me being here is not so pleasant."

Puzzled, she gestured to a chair. "Please sit."

He took a chair and sat for a moment brushing creases from the sleeves of his jacket, and it seemed to Camilla that he was thinking about how to phrase what he had to say. This was new. Before, in every situation where they had met, whether it be on government business or in a social setting, he had been quick witted and never stuck for words, his use of English as impeccable as his suit.

"What can I do for you, Ambassador?"

Giacomo's expression, normally inscrutable, had a look of concern. They'd had many meetings during her four years as the Home Secretary, and some of them had been quite difficult. But even during these challenging meetings, he was always charming and affable while putting his government's point of view across. He was a consummate professional diplomat. But not right now.

He uncharacteristically cleared his throat, coughing into his fist, there was another pause while he was obviously thinking of how to best phrase what he had to say. Eventually, he fixed his gaze on her. "We are aware that there is a campaign on the coast of East Anglia to get an area renamed, or at least, returned to its original name. Are we correct?"

"Yes, that is correct, campaigners want the wooded area of Southmere changed back to Twinmere, the original name of the village that was lost to the sea centuries ago."

Moretti had a look of concern mixed with disappointment. "The change, is it likely to happen?"

"Yes, probably. They have presented a strong case and have produced a map that predates all others. It is being looked at by my department and they have indicated to me that there is no reason that the change shouldn't go ahead." She shrugged slightly, and for a moment, she thought she saw his shoulders drop a fraction. "It is just the change of a name of a sparsely populated region. Although it's known as a village, only the wood remains, the dwellings were never rebuilt and the only people that live there are holiday makers during the summer. Changing the name is trivial, and as you can imagine, it is not the most pressing item on my agenda."

"No, Home Secretary, it is far from trivial." His voice was firm with a touch of disquiet, his expression serious and a total contrast to his usual calm, measured manner. His use of 'Home Secretary' instead of her name indicated the seriousness of his visit. "We feel that it is vitally important that the name is not changed."

She shook her head, confused at his statement and demeanour. "Why is this so important to the Italian government?"

"It is not my government that is concerned, Camilla. Please indulge me for a moment."

She frowned; Giacomo was not his usual self, so she decided to hear what he had to say. "Go on."

"You have had two deaths, a nine-year-old boy and a forty-four-year-old woman. Both went missing at night, both were discovered the next day, or at least, their skeletons were found, devoid of all flesh."

She shuddered inside as she recalled the descriptions of what was left of Darren Turner and Celia Jones. "Sadly, that is correct."

"And your police have no suspect, or suspects."

She decided on the diplomatic answer, as she was unwilling to admit failings to a foreign diplomat, albeit one from a friendly country and a person she considered as much of a friend as protocol allowed. "Police investigations are ongoing." Even before the words left her mouth, she knew he would see through them.

His face darkened. "You will never find the being that did it."

Camilla frowned deeply, further confused at his choice of the word, 'being'. It was an odd thing for him to say, and she had never heard him slip up before. "The being?" she asked incredulously. "What do you mean when you say 'the being'? Surely you mean the person, or persons?"

Moretti dodged the question. "The Moreno family tree can trace a direct line back to the thirteenth century, and it is probably the oldest family in Spain. Some of your ancestors held positions in the Holy Roman Catholic church, many became bishops, two became cardinals, many others became emissaries or diplomats. Your family is still closely connected to the church." He nodded to the rosary at the side of her desk, then to the cross on the wall, and a well-used Bible on a bookshelf. "And you, yourself, are known to be devout."

"All of that is correct and I have made no secret of my devotion. But what does this have to do with the naming of an insignificant village in Suffolk and the two murders? And why is it so vitally important?"

"The village name is far from insignificant, and it is of vital importance to the safety of your citizens." He handed over a letter. "We are relying on your faith; this will explain everything." As she took it, she noticed the crossed keys and crown that was the coat of arms of the Holy See and Vatican City.

"It is from Cardinal Visconti, he leads the office for the maintenance of the continuity. It is a powerful office." He fixed a hard stare on her. "Do not read the letter aloud, do not ever utter any of its contents!" he warned forcefully.

Still confused, but trying hard not to show it, she opened the letter and started to read. He saw her eyes opening wide as she read. The letter detailed every account of the Twinmere beast, from the first written record in the tenth century right up to the present day, and how the beast would take anyone who said its name. It included details of the bishop's conference that ordered all references to the village name to be changed and the destruction of the village that followed.

She put the letter down and sat open-mouthed for a few moments. "Has the Italian government always known about this?"

"My government knows nothing of this. I am not here on government business, I am here on the instruction of Cardinal Visconti, I am a member of the office for the maintenance of the continuity. The bishops were right to have the name changed, but if it returns to its former name, then the beast could be set free again. It would only take one person to post its name on social media, and given the low intelligence of some people, it would probably become the 'name the beast challenge'." He sneered slightly as he said it, another break in his usual calm demeanour that surprised her. He paused and sighed. "The beast cannot be stopped, in the ninth century whole armies were set against it, but it attacked at night under cover of darkness, it is always at night. A trap would be set and a volunteer would say its name, this was considered a great honour, but the beast was sly. Many died trying to fight it."

"If that was the case, why is there nothing about it in history books?"

"The bishops had every reference to it destroyed and people were forbidden to talk about it, so the history died out, but the beast didn't. The only way to be safe is to make sure it is never called, so that is why it is absolutely vital that the name doesn't change. We understand that there is only one ancient map that records the region as Twinmere, and this has been the driver for the campaign."

Camilla sat processing everything she had learned over the past few minutes, trying hard not let it show just how shocked she was. "You said this is about the safety of the citizens of my country; could it become an international issue?"

"With the exception of these recent tragic incidents, the last time the beast was called there was no effective international communication for ordinary citizens. No internet, no mobile phone network, no international TV broadcasts, no mass international travel. Now there is all of that, and one person can potentially broadcast to millions in an instant and each one of them can retransmit the message to a million more. We don't know if the beast can cross water, there has never been any record of that, so we don't know if it could become an issue for countries outside of the United Kingdom."

Camilla took a moment to think of all the implications, subconsciously reaching over and taking hold of her rosary. "I will block the name change, but there are some strong voices in the campaign, so I will need a credible reason to do it."

"We are aware of all the players in the campaign, and yes, some are powerful, but we can help you there. The Vatican has the world's best document analysts and conservators, they will take the document and declare it to be a seventeenth century forgery. I would recommend that due to the actual age of the document, the British government should request that it is kept in the Vatican vaults in perpetuity to prevent deterioration. Certain elements will of course challenge this, but the Vatican has been challenged many time before—this does not concern us."

"What will actually happen to the map?"

"It will be destroyed. Cardinal Visconti asserts that while antiquities should always be preserved, this map is too dangerous to be allowed to exist, and I agree with him."

Camilla nodded, accepting and agreeing with his point of view. "I will obtain the map; how long will the 'analysis' take?"

"I'd say that three weeks would be a credible period for the analysis to be concluded."

Camilla thought for a moment. "We'll time the announcement to coincide with a three-day climate change conference in London, and it is known that there will be large demonstrations all over the country before, during and after the conference, and all the usual suspects have announced that they will be blocking roads in every county in the country. That will clog up all the news feeds, so an announcement on the document will in all likelihood not even be reported."

He nodded approvingly. "That is a good idea."

Camilla's shock and horror at what she had been made aware of faded and her organising brain took over, quickly running through various scenarios of how to deal with the campaign organisers. "I will arrange a low-key operation that expresses regret that the ancient hoax has wasted so many well-meaning people's time. They actually worked quite hard, so I'll meet them—pressing the flesh always diffuses controversies."

He looked at her curiously. "Forgive me for saying this, Camilla, but I have to say things as how they are, for everyone's sake."

She smiled, well aware of the subject he was going to bring up.

"Polls suggest that your party may lose the next election. Should that happen, can you ensure that your successor will not reverse your decision out of spite?"

Camilla half-laughed. "It is not a question of *may* lose, but *will* lose. We are well aware that we'll be wiped out. Which is why I am using our majority to push through necessary legislation that is seen as highly unpopular, even though the electorate fails to see that it's all in their best interest. Rest assured, Giacomo, I know who my successor is likely to be, and he will expend vast amounts of energy correcting my 'terrible' policies, as he has called them many times in the media. If he starts to look into the name change, I will accuse him of triviality, I will use it to undermine him; after all, that's what the other side have accused me of."

"Thank you for your time, Camilla. Now, please indulge me one more time; only three people know of the existence of this letter, the cardinal, myself and now you. No one else can ever know of this, the letter must be destroyed, and I must witness its destruction."

She took the letter and placed it into a level P-7 high-security shredder, its blades slicing the paper into tiny rectangles of less than one millimetre by five millimetres.

The last of the document disappeared into the machine and the whirring stopped. She looked at him then gestured to the machine. "I will make sure that the grindings are incinerated." She paused and thought about her words and whether she should say what she wanted him to know. She decided that he had the right to hear what she had to say.

"My duty is to my country, and every minute of every day, I do my duty to the best of my abilities, but my loyalty is to my church. The letter never existed, and although I cannot deny that our meeting took place, this particular conversation never happened."

Giacomo nodded in appreciation. "Thank you, now I must report this back to Cardinal Visconti right away. Good day, Camilla, and thank you for your time and your loyalty."

Within days, the box holding the map was being fed into a grinder in a room beneath the Vatican. A month later, Camilla had met with and shaken hands with Margo and the other organisers of the campaign, commending them on the work that they had done while expressing her disappointment that the map had been a fake. Some made a half-hearted effort at maintaining the campaign, but Sir James and all the other serious voices went on to other projects, where their personal cachet would yield more positive results. Without Margo's driving force, continuing the campaign was always doomed to failure.

Within two months, all efforts to keep the campaign alive had fizzled out and the legend of the name consigned to an obscure footnote in history. Though due to a clause in the contract with the manufacturers, the local council still had to pay the sign makers for all the road signs that had been ordered, even though none had been made.

Five months later, there was a general election and as every poll predicted, the governing party was thrashed, with over two hundred of their MPs losing their seats, including Camilla's, a seat that she had held with a comfortable majority for the past four elections. She didn't really care, she'd grown tired of politics with its oft-sinister skulduggery, intrigue and backstabbing. And despite the hard outer shell that she had developed, the constant personal attacks and accusations of hypocrisy for introducing laws to halt economic migration, while herself being the product of economic migration, were starting to get to her. She was glad to be out and back in the world that was her first love, business. Her salary as a board member of a civil engineering firm was nearly ten times that of her parliamentary pay, and she started to think about going to Italy and maybe buying some clothes from the designer that Giacomo always went to.

Chapter 17
A Trip to the Beach

One Year After Darren's Death

Both the Darren Turner and Celia Jones cases were still open but had long since been officially listed as cold. Buckley and Griffin had met a few times, both expressing their growing depression over their failure to solve the cases. Buckley had floated the idea of an unknown animal, admitting that he'd not mentioned it to anyone else for fear of ridicule. At first Griffin seemed responsive, but the more they talked it over, the more unlikely it obviously was to the two men. Eventually, Buckley had to admit that it was a fanciful idea born out of his frustration.

The Gupta family were visiting the beach at Southmere for the first time; it had been recommended by friends, and the parents liked the fact that there was nothing really there except for a tea shop. No garish amusement arcade, no candyfloss stalls or chip shops, and most importantly for Janani, the mother, there were no loud drunks to spoil the day as had happen the last time they went to the seaside. The only other people were families just like hers enjoying the fresh air and wide open space. There were just the cliffs, the shingle beach and the north sea. Amal, the father, was keen that his three boys should stay away from trivial things, and they were too young to care, their only complaint was that the sea was cold, and that it would be difficult to play cricket on the stony beach.

"Why don't you explore while your mother gets dinner ready?"

All three ran off to see if they could find anything interesting and were soon back, carrying odd-shaped stones and bits of bleached driftwood. Rayaan, the youngest of the sons, handed the father a piece of weathered paper with numbers barely visible.

"This was in the grass, it looks like a code."

"Maybe it's a code that will give directions to a treasure chest that's been buried by pirates!"

The boy became excited, his eyes opening wide. "Can you work out the code?"

"I'll do it when we get home."

"Can't you do it now?" he whined.

Amal folded the paper and put it in his pocket. "I deal with numbers all day, every day, besides, I want to have a paddle in the sea."

"It's really cold."

"Cold? Well, you say it's cold, but I'm not bothered by the cold." Amal made a show of taking off his shoes and socks and rolling up his trousers then wading into the water, quickly turning around and walking out, with his wife chuckling to herself as she watched his expression change.

"Well, is it cold?" Janani smirked as he got back to her.

"Yes, very!"

She got out her phone and looked up the average temperature for the north sea. "Hmm, it should be around fourteen to sixteen degrees."

"Humpf," he grunted, feigning disbelief. "It felt a lot colder. So much for global warming that is supposed to be heating up the seas."

"It's never going to be as warm as you like your baths to be."

The family stayed at the beach until four then made the two-hour drive back to the outskirts of Leagrave just to the north of Luton.

The boys were in bed and Amal and his wife were relaxing. Janani was on social media posting pictures of their day out while her husband was replying to some work emails. He finished, then took the paper from his pocket. Janani looked up over the top of her iPad to see him rolling his fingers one at a time while muttering the letters of the alphabet.

"Are you trying to do that in your head?"

"Yes. I have the first three letters, twenty, eight and five. That's T, H, E."

"Writing it down would be easier," she laughed and went back to her iPad.

"Where's the fun in that?" he chuckled.

Ten minutes later, he had finished.

Janani noticed the puzzled look on his face. "Well, what is it? What does it say?"

He frowned slightly. "Nothing really, it just says 'The Twinmere Beast'." He chucked the paper in a bin.

Janani shrugged. "I read that some people thought that Twinmere was the original name of Southmere."

One hundred and twenty miles away, vapour rose from the ground and started to drift west. Once again, it travelled through the countryside at night, staying away from the bright lights of towns and villages.

Camilla sat stunned as she read the news report; a father of three went missing, only to have his skeleton found three days later, picked clean of all flesh. A panicked phone call to Giacomo confirmed what she already knew to be true; they were impotent in the face of this danger and that she could never tell anyone about it.

"We have to accept, Camilla, that there is nothing we can do. The name is out there now. All we can hope for is that no one else ever speaks its name."

Four days after Amal's skeleton was found, a worker sorting through paper at the recycling centre saw the note with the numbers. Intrigued at what looked like a code, and being a curious type, he picked it up and put it in his pocket.

"I'll work out what that is later," he muttered to himself as he carried on with his task. He forgot about it and the paper was destroyed when his wife washed his clothes.

Chapter 18
Christina

A sullen, subdued Christina entered Helmwood police station, though this time it was of her own volition, instead of yet another arrest for shoplifting. It was two years since her mother's death and the family had completely fallen apart. Buckley had visited the home on many occasions and had seen the rapid decline. Clutter and mess had quickly built up, with unopened mail lying around, unwashed clothes strewn everywhere and mouldy food on plates piled up in the sink.

Richard had swiftly descended deep into alcoholism, Oliver had tried to keep the family together but had developed a drug habit. He had been arrested for dealing cannabis a couple of times and it was obvious to Buckley that sooner or later, probably sooner, Oliver would see the inside of a prison cell. Christina had turned to petty crime and had moved out of the formerly immaculate family home and was in a relationship with an older woman, living with her in a run-down area on the outskirts of Helmwood.

Of all the family members, it was Christina that concerned him the most. She'd taken up smoking at fifteen and was up to forty a day before switching to roll-ups. She had withdrawn into herself almost immediately after her mother's death. She hardly spoke, and when she did, her sentences were punctuated with obscenities, and it was ugly to hear the 'C' word repeated so often from such a young girl. Richard had been too drunk to correct her and Oliver didn't seem to care.

Buckley didn't need to be a psychologist to understand that all of this was the product of unresolved grief. He felt it too, he felt it keenly. His failure to find the killer and bring closure to the family was a burden that he carried and he felt that this was just as damaging to the family as Celia's murder was, maybe even more so.

He ignored the tattoo on Christina's throat that extended up to her jawline and the row of five small stars around her left eye, even though she was sixteen and getting the tattoo was illegal. He knew she'd probably lied about her age, and given the below average quality of the ink work, it would have been done by a less than diligent back street tattooist. There was no point to him asking who it was, she would never tell him.

He braced himself for abuse. "What do you want to talk to me about, Christina?" Abuse didn't come.

Christina sighed and stared at the floor for a few moments. "What she said seemed to be important to you; you asked Oliver if she'd said anything about a monster, he told me and I blanked it out because I thought it was fuckin' stupid, and I forgot about it because of the situation, but I remembered it this morning."

He picked up on her use of 'she' rather than 'Mum' and that bothered him—the bond was permanently broken now. "What did she say, Christina?"

"We'd been helping her do a crossword; she filled in the last three clues and said, 'The Twinmere beast, there, all done'

...then she muttered something about it sounding like a monster. Four days later, she was gone. So, now you know, but it ain't gonna fuckin' bring her back, is it?" she mumbled as she turned and left.

Four days later, Christina's skeleton was found by some dog-walkers.